Ready for contact

If Nona hadn't known better, she'd have thought Nicholas was watching her. Utterly impossible. Still, she had to make sure. She turned—and there he was, leaning against a tree, arms folded, staring at her.

"For heaven's sake," she said. She dusted the snow from her pants, paying no attention to what she was doing because her gaze never left him. He definitely looked male. Suddenly she realized she should have purchased and worn the sexy green ski outfit.

"What are you doing here? And don't tell me this is fate or destiny."

"I followed your tracks," he answered, eyes sparkling.

Nona shivered, even though she wasn't cold. Instead she felt warm, very warm. She smiled, then held her breath when he started walking toward her.

He was going to kiss her!

Dear Reader,

Welcome to Silhouette—experience the magic of the wonderful world where two people fall in love. Meet heroines who will make you cheer for their happiness, and heroes (be they the boy next door or a handsome, mysterious stranger) who will win your heart. Silhouette Romance reflects the magic of love—sweeping you away with books that will make you laugh and cry, heartwarming, poignant stories that will move you time and time again.

In the coming months we're publishing romances by many of your all-time favorites, such as Diana Palmer, Brittany Young, Sondra Stanford and Annette Broadrick. Your response to these authors and our other Silhouette Romance authors has served as a touchstone for us, and we're pleased to bring you more books with Silhouette's distinctive medley of charm, wit and—above all—*romance*.

I hope you enjoy this book and the many stories to come. Experience the magic!

Sincerely,

Tara Hughes
Senior Editor
Silhouette Books

MARCINE SMITH

The Perfect Wife

Published by Silhouette Books New York

America's Publisher of Contemporary Romance

For Daryl

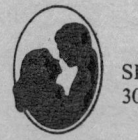

SILHOUETTE BOOKS
300 E. 42nd St., New York, N.Y. 10017

Copyright © 1989 by Marcine C. Smith

All rights reserved. Except for use in any review, the reproduction or utilization of this work in whole or in part in any form by any electronic, mechanical or other means, now known or hereafter invented, including xerography, photocopying and recording, or in any information storage or retrieval system, is forbidden without the permission of Silhouette Books, 300 E. 42nd St., New York, N.Y. 10017

ISBN: 0-373-08683-0

First Silhouette Books printing November 1989

All the characters in this book are fictitious. Any resemblance to actual persons, living or dead, is purely coincidental.

®: Trademark used under license and registered in the United States Patent and Trademark Office and in other countries.

Printed in the U.S.A.

Books by Marcine Smith

Silhouette Desire

Never a Stranger #364

Silhouette Romance

Murphy's Law #589
Waltz with the Flowers #659
The Perfect Wife #683

MARCINE SMITH

lives on a farm in northwest Iowa with her husband and three of their four sons. She loves reading, writing romances, watching baseball, basketball and football, long drives through the Iowa-South Dakota countryside and the smell of freshly mowed hay. But her favorite things are sharing the porch swing with her husband at dusk on a summer's day, watching the sun set and listening to the corn grow.

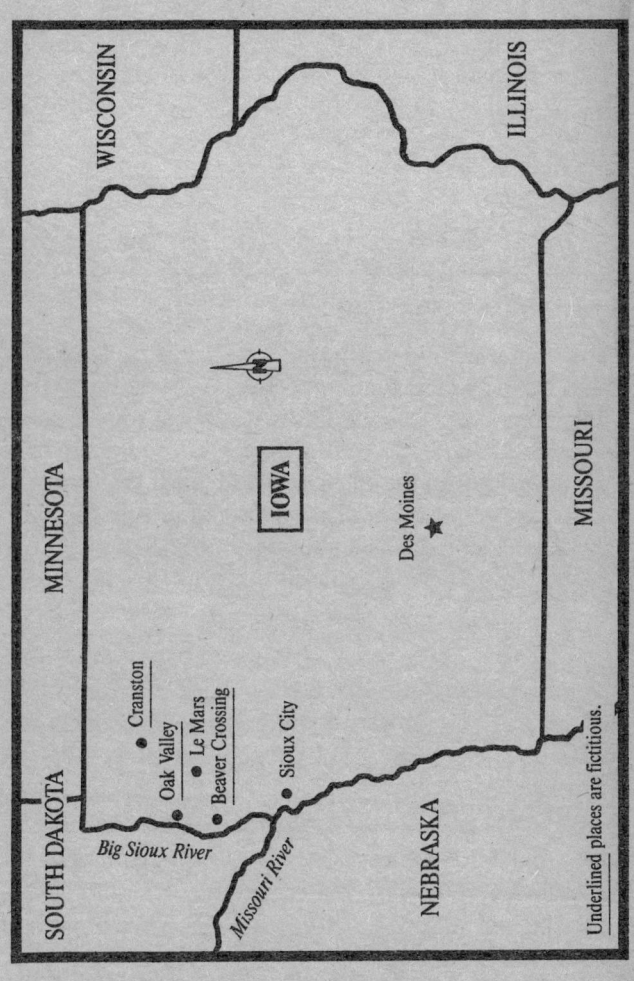

Chapter One

Nona Alexander and her assistant coach, Mel Baldwin, stood on the sidelines watching the Beaver Crossing girls' basketball team warm up before their first game of the season.

"The girls look sharp," Nona said.

"The new warm-up suits are sharp," Mel drawled. "Gold and black together is sharp. Or I could say that this is Friday night and if you'll give me the weekend to consider whether or not the girls are sharp, I'd appreciate it."

"Pessimist," she said. She crossed her arms and gave him a look. In spite of his grumbling, he was a sweetheart. When Nona had inherited the coaching job, he had volunteered to assist her even though he knew this would be a rebuilding year and that wins would be hard to come by.

He had a right to be pessimistic about their chances of winning tonight, Nona admitted. They were at a disadvantage. They were playing Cranston on Cranston's home court, and Cranston's starting players were experienced seniors. Beaver Crossing boasted one senior on their twelve-girl roster.

But these girls were special. They worked hard. And they would always play their hearts out. That was all she and Mel could ask of them, Nona was thinking when she got the overpowering feeling that someone was staring at her.

Silly notion, she told herself. Several hundred pairs of eyes had likely inspected her already. Still, the urge to turn toward where she felt the gaze coming from was irresistible. Slowly, she glanced over her shoulder and met the gaze of a tall referee.

She couldn't see the color of his eyes, but talk about a penetrating look. She went from a toasty warmth to instant simmer before smiling self-consciously and turning away.

Being singled out in a crowded room, let alone a basketball court didn't happen to her. She had likely imagined the gaze's intensity. The urge to peek and check out the man was hard to deny, but she resisted the temptation.

Instead she watched as Cara, a freshman player, somehow bounced the basketball off her knee into the lap of a little boy sitting in the bleachers twenty feet away. The boy's bag of popcorn popped from his hand, and the contents spilled on the floor. He looked at Cara accusingly. Cara hid her face in her hands.

Nona called softly, "Cara. Come here." When Cara was standing before her, Nona placed her fingers under the girl's chin and gently raised her head. "Don't worry about it. Pregame jitters, that's all." She patted Cara's shoulder comfortingly.

"I don't know, Mrs. Alexander," the blond-haired girl said. "I feel sick."

"You'll be okay once the game starts. Believe me. I've been through it." Nona felt a prickling sensation on her spine. He was looking at her again! She squeezed Cara's shoulder. "I have confidence in you," she added.

Cara trotted off. Nona glanced over her shoulder and caught him looking at her. He smiled sheepishly, then turned so she saw his profile. He was handsome and rugged in build. Shrugging, Nona tried to dismiss the nagging distraction.

"So the girls are sharp, are they?" Mel muttered. "We'll be lucky to come out of this alive." He scanned the other team. "Look at that!" he exclaimed, staring at two Cranston players who were over six feet tall.

"I see," Nona said. Beaver Crossing didn't have a six-footer. "We'll do all right," she stated firmly.

He was looking at her again! She didn't have to see to confirm it. It was terribly disconcerting. Flattering, too. But she wished he would stop, at least until after the game.

"Kendrick," Arlo Sparks said, his voice raised to be heard over the cheerleaders and crowd. "I have the feeling you haven't been listening to me."

Nicholas grinned. The moment he had stepped into the gymnasium, he had noticed Mrs. Alexander, a tall and voluptuous woman with thick hair that fell in waves to her shoulder. Her physical appearance had drawn his attention at first, but it was what had happened when her gaze met his that kept him looking back at her. He had the strangest feeling he knew her.

"I couldn't help but notice the relationship Mrs. Alexander has with her girls," Nicholas said. "Like the way she comforted the young lady."

"I'm sure her relationship with her girls is what you've been staring at." Arlo laughed.

"All right. In addition to noticing how she handles her girls, the truth is I have the feeling I know her." Embarrassed, Nicholas raked his fingers through his hair. He didn't make a habit of admiring good-looking women.

"I doubt Nona's ever been to Texas. And since you've only been in Iowa a short time—" Arlo's expression was wry "—if you try handing a line like that to her, she'll laugh in your face, my friend."

"Nona." Nicholas said. "You know Mrs. Alexander?"

"Haven't seen her in years—but do I know her!" Arlo's blue eyes brightened. "She was the love of my life when I was twelve. Then my folks moved from Beaver Crossing to Sioux City. Didn't get over Nona until I was thirteen."

Nicholas laughed. He had met Arlo a week ago when the referees and substitutes hired by the Two Rivers Conference had held their preseason meeting. He was refereeing tonight because Arlo's regular partner was ill. Nicholas knew they would work well together because they had taken an immediate liking to each other.

Nicholas wondered what Nona Alexander had looked like as a girl. Long pigtails slapping her back? Her teeth in braces? It was hard to imagine after seeing her now, wearing tailored green slacks and a matching light green sweater. The clothes were practical, yet they flattered the curves of her body. "From what I can observe, I'd venture she was worth a crush at age twelve."

"Crush? No way, Nicholas. I said love, I meant love," Arlo wisecracked. Then he turned serious. "At twelve, Nona was nearly as tall as she is now—and skinny. She laughed when the kids called her bean pole or skeleton, but fought like a bantam hen protecting a clutch when kids started picking on the underdogs, those who were too slow, too fat, too shy. I was stupid and fat, but Nona made me feel special. Good about myself, if you know what I mean."

"I know what you mean," Nicholas said. It had always seemed to him that some people were born with that ability, while others had to work to achieve it.

"I hear through the grapevine she still has a soft spot for the underdogs. I've been told she'd offered to take the coaching job because the talent graduated and no one else would put his neck on the line working with the girls."

Nicholas had to ask. "What's her husband like?"

Arlo frowned. "Jon? What can I say about Jon that will be objective? Even at twelve Jon was tall, blond, brilliant. He was liked by every girl in school."

"Not your best buddy?" Nicholas smiled.

"Strangely enough, I liked Jon. He had a way about him that made you overlook his faults."

"Faults like being tall, blond and brilliant," Nicholas offered.

"Exactly." Arlo shook his head. "Nona and Jon are divorced. Rumor has it Jon wanted to play the field. I'm kind of inclined to believe that's what happened because Nona's the kind who'd stick otherwise."

Nicholas didn't comment. Arlo might believe Nona Alexander was without fault, and she could be, but when it came to a failed marriage, Nicholas knew from personal experience that there were always two sides to the story.

"Tell you what," Arlo said. "I'm feeling generous tonight, so why don't I amble over, say hello to the Cranston coach and snag their captain. You amble over, introduce yourself to Nona and grab Beaver Crossing's captain. Meet you at center court."

"Sounds good," Nicholas said.

Arlo winked and walked away, leaving Nicholas free to do what he had been wanting to do—approach Nona Alexander. At the moment her back was to him, her attention on the girls as they continued to warm up.

She was only a couple of inches shorter than his six-feet height, he noticed as he walked toward her. But what color were her eyes?

"Mrs. Alexander?"

Nona had felt him coming, and had known before he spoke that his voice would be low and strong. She wondered if he would live up to what she was visualizing. Maybe his teeth would be crooked, his lips thin and unexpressive, and his dark complexion, so attractive from a distance, would reveal he needed a shave.

She turned. He was hazel-eyed, with thick, black brows and lashes. He had asked her a question. "I am Mrs. Alexander," she answered in a rush.

Lovely contralto, Nicholas reflected. Her eyes were light blue and iridescent. But he wasn't poetic. He didn't know how to describe her eyes except to think they were a work of art, framed by black lashes.

"I'm Nicholas Kendrick," he said, extending his hand.

As Nona took it, her gaze dropped to his left hand. Tanned, with a pale circle on his ring finger. He had been wearing a wedding band. Or still was and had simply forgotten it tonight.

She lifted her gaze, pulled her hand from the warmth of his. "I'm Nona," she said.

"Nona. I've been told you'll laugh if I say this, but I feel as if I should recognize you."

So the intense look hadn't been dark at all, but pondering. She was a case of mistaken identity. She had to admit she felt a stab of disappointment.

"It sounds like a line, but I believe you," she said.

"So have I met you before?"

Nona smiled. Had she met him, his rugged appearance might have faded from memory, but never *the look*. "I'm sure you haven't."

"At least you didn't laugh," Nicholas said. "I'll be sharing the refereeing duties with Arlo Sparks tonight. I believe you know Arlo."

The Cranston band began playing its school song; both squads of cheerleaders went into dance routines. The gym was vibrating with noise.

"Arlo Sparks is here?" she asked, leaning around Nicholas. She saw Arlo looking in their direction, smiling. She returned the smile, tossed him a little wave and straightened.

"I'd heard Arlo was going to be one of the conference referees this year, but I haven't seen him in such a long time. He looks fantastic."

Her expression was open, allowing Nicholas to gaze deeply into her eyes. He marked no skittishness, no pretense; instead he could see her taking up lost causes.

"Arlo said he was in love with you," he offered.

Nona smiled. "Arlo was in love with every girl in school at one time or another."

Nicholas thought her smile was very beautiful. Reluctantly, he glanced at the clock on the score board. Three minutes to the buzzer. Hardly enough time to exchange life histories.

"I'm new to northwest Iowa," he said.

"I'd never have guessed." Nona chuckled. "Where in the south did you live?"

"Texas," Nicholas said.

"Great state, Texas. Cowboys and all."

"Great state, Iowa. Coaches and all. I'm living near Oak Valley right now."

Whatever Nona had been feeling in the mesmerizing last few moments disappeared. Jon's parents farmed near Oak Valley. She hadn't seen them since the divorce had become final. She believed they had never forgiven her for leaving Jon.

She forced what she hoped would appear to be a natural smile. "I know quite a few people in the Oak Valley area," she said. "Excuse me, please. I'd like to speak to my mother before the game starts. Our captain is Kate Breemer, number 11."

Nona beckoned to Kate, introduced her to Nicholas and made her escape to the end of the bleachers where her mother was sitting in her wheelchair.

Jenny Niles was an energetic sixty. She suffered from a crippling form of rheumatoid arthritis and when the disease flared, she used a wheelchair rather than restrict herself to her home.

"Handsome referee," Jenny said, giving Nona a rascally grin.

"Aren't you too old to be noticing something like that, Mother?"

Jenny laughed hoarsely. "The last time I checked, I only had one foot in the grave, and the other one was doing a fox trot. Of course I noticed. I've never seen him before. What's his name?"

"Nicholas Kendrick. He's from Texas. And he has a voice that goes with the build. Deep, melodious, kind of rumbles in his chest."

"I think I'll call the young man over and give him my telephone number."

"Forget it, Mother. He's probably married."

"You talked to him two, three minutes and you didn't ask? What kind of woman did I raise?"

"You raised a lady, Mother, and ladies don't run around saying, 'By the way, I notice you aren't wearing a wedding ring...but are you married?'"

Jenny gave Nona the eye. "No wedding ring, huh? Then march back over there and check it out."

"Sure thing, Mother. I'll do that."

"So don't, Nona Marilee. I've seen enough already to allow me to do a little fantasizing," Jenny said.

Nona leaned down to whisper, "You do that, Mother, but I'll pester you until you tell me what kind of fantasies you had."

Jenny chuckled. "You want a fantasy life, get your own."

Nona had looked into Nicholas's eyes, questioned what she saw, wondered if it had meaning. Was that fantasy? On her part, maybe. On his part, it had merely been a case of mistaken identity.

Nona lightly kissed Jenny's temple, then straightened, hand on hips. "Will you be able to see all right from here?"

"Don't worry about me," Jenny said. She raised her hands and spread her fingers. "I'm ready."

"Ready for what, for heaven's sake?"

"For one of Cara's knee passes."

Nona laughed. The buzzer rang. "I'll see you after the game," she said, then hurried to join the huddle. She wanted to give the girls some last-minute instructions. And maybe she'd offer a silent prayer.

"Un-be-liev-able!" As she stood, Nona shoved her sweater sleeves up, pushed her bottom lip out, then blew her bangs from her forehead. "Kate! Call time out," she yelled. "Kendrick is blind," she muttered to Mel. "Absolutely, undeniably blind!"

"Keep this up and you're going to get a technical," Mel warned, referring to the three times Nona had jumped to her feet out of the coaching box in silent protest over Kendrick's calling fouls on Kate.

With less than two minutes left, Cranston was leading Beaver Crossing by five points and Nicholas had just called another foul on Kate.

The crowd roar was deafening. As the girls trotted toward the sidelines, Nona said, "Mel, I'm going to have a word with Kendrick."

Mel nodded. Nona stepped toward the scorers' bench and beckoned to Nicholas.

He handed the basketball to Arlo, then walked over. "I gather you'd like clarification on the last call," he said when he stood before her.

"Clarification?" Nona said calmly. "All night long I've refrained—with a great deal of effort—from saying anything. However! There was no way that Kate could have committed that last foul."

"Mrs. Alexander, I am normally unemotional in situations like this, but you have been verbally attacking me all night long."

"I have not! You've not heard *one* word from me."

"I've *read* your lips!"

"I doubt that," Nona rebutted, desperately hoping he hadn't. She had whispered some truly unforgivable things.

"Your reference to my character was bad enough without the looks—"

"The looks?" Nona echoed. He was leaning toward her. New sensations surged through her body. Crazy thoughts whirled through her head, none of which had anything to do with basketball! She had to resist the impulse to place her fingers on his chest; she didn't even know whether she wanted to touch him or push him away.

"Yes, looks. Admonishing, insulting looks," Nicholas said. "Now Kate may move like a butterfly and sting—"

"I don't think this situation calls for poetry, Mr. Kendrick," Nona interrupted, indignant.

"Nor do I especially," Nicholas said. "I was trying to make the point that you lack objectivity."

His words hit the bull's-eye, Nona admitted. She wasn't objective. But how could she be objective? Her girls were playing as hard as they could and weren't getting a break on the officiating. She didn't like being aggressive, but as the coach it was her duty to question calls.

"That I'm not objective is your opinion, sir. An opinion which I feel obligated to point out is also without objectivity," she said, sounding determined.

His eyes darkened. "From where *I* made the call, it was obvious Kate made a foul."

"Would you mind if I inquire how long you've been a referee?" she asked starchily.

"Long enough," he said. "However in Texas we play five-girl ball. This is my first six-girl game."

"Would you mind if I said that's obvious?" Nona asked in her best sarcastic tone. "Or if I say stick to refereeing games in the larger schools where they play five-man ball."

"Yes, I would mind. And I'm going to plant a technical on you if this kind of thing keeps up."

"Your call was wrong."

"I called it as I saw it, Mrs. Alexander. And you are out of the coaching box for the fourth time tonight." He pointed to her feet.

"Well," Nona scoffed even though he was right. She was well beyond the area of the coaching box. "I'm surprised you noticed a little thing so close like that considering how farsighted you seem to be."

She was immediately appalled with herself. She never lost her temper. Well, she lost it, but she never got angry. Well, she did get angry, but she was never unreasonable and angry at the same time. Darn him, anyway.

"Did you just call me blind, Mrs. Alexander?" he asked ominously.

Nona hurriedly stepped back into the coaching box. "I didn't mean it."

"I hate to do this. I really do. But you've been asking for it all night long." He turned to the scorer. "Technical on the Beaver Crossing bench."

The Cranston supporters went wild. The Beaver Crossing supporters booed, and Nona, thoroughly bemused by her behavior, sank to the bench. What a way to start her coaching career! With a technical! And worse than her personal embarrassment, it could cost the girls the game. Now Cranston was getting two free shots, after which they'd have possession of the ball.

It was Kendrick's fault, Nona thought glumly. He was the cause of all her problems tonight. She had been too aware of him and his gaze, which, it turned out, had *not* been intended for her! Then his mention of Oak Valley had set her on edge.

She leaned to Mel and whispered, "I can't believe I did that."

"Don't let it get to you. The girls are really fired up now," Mel observed.

The subs were screaming at the top of their voices. The Cranston band was playing a fight song. Cheerleaders had everyone in the bleachers standing and chanting, "Fight! Fight! Fight!" And there were little creatures in her head doing just that, Nona thought as she rubbed her temples.

Cranston seventy-eight. Beaver Crossing seventy-three.

Nona shook hands with the Cranston coach and each of the Cranston girls, then huddled her girls. She told them they had scored a moral victory in playing Cranston so tightly on Cranston's home floor.

The Beaver Crossing team, smiling, left for the locker room. Nona started to follow, only to find Nicholas blocking her path.

"Your girls show promise, Mrs. Alexander. But before they can reach potential, you're going to have to do something about Kate's habit of charging," he offered.

"Habit of charging," Nona repeated. "Actually, I do intend to do something about it." She smiled brilliantly. "I intend to go home and pray that my girls never play another game refereed by someone who calls a charge the way you do."

He grinned. "You'll need to do a lot of praying, Nona."

The dark flecks in his hazel eyes danced and Nona wanted to warm to his lightheartedness. But there was a sense of uneasiness in her that she couldn't overcome.

She smiled. "I'll use a pillow, Nicholas," she said, then turned and walked away.

Chapter Two

When Nona walked into Irene's café the next morning just before nine and was greeted by a round of applause, she knew the scuttlebutt about the technical had already made the rounds. To say that news traveled fast in Beaver Crossing was an understatement.

She acknowledged the clamor and the calls of "Way to go, Nona!" with a smile and a wave. She was also blushing and vainly trying to look inconspicuous.

After visiting briefly with several friends, she sat on a stool at the counter and waited for Irene to bring Marsha Wilm's breakfast.

Marsha was an elderly spinster who'd fallen some months ago, broken her hip and was confined to her house. Jenny usually picked up Marsha's meals and took them to her, but until Jenny was mobile again,

Nona was doing the run on weekends, and on the other days Irene grabbed anyone available.

"So, you got slapped with a T last night," Irene said, chuckling as she placed a container before Nona.

"Believe me, it will never happen again," Nona said.

"Well, maybe it should. You allow people to take advantage of your good nature."

Nona winced inwardly at Irene's offhand comment. She had been called good-natured for as long as she could remember. Even after Jon had told her that he had fallen out of love with her and in love with his secretary, he had made a point of telling her she was good-natured but lacked the "fire" Joann had. Well, something about Kendrick had brought out the fire in her. She'd had enough fire for ten people.

"No one could have called me good-natured last night, Irene," she admitted. "I definitely lost my cool, as the kids would say."

"Hear it was the new ref who gave you the T," Irene said.

Nona had dreamed about Nicholas. Or had it been a nightmare? All she remembered was she'd yelled over and over again, "How can such beautiful eyes be blind?" and Nicholas, his eyes holding her with their mesmerizing spell, kept throwing her out of the ball game.

"Your mom says he looked like a Texas cowboy," Irene continued, her round face breaking into a tickled smile.

"For goodness sake, when did you talk to Mother?"

"About five minutes ago. She called to tell me you were on your way over to pick up Marsha's breakfast," Irene answered. "Jenny said the Texan was as blind as a bat but good to look at. Said she spent the whole game wishing she was a couple of years younger."

"Mother shows every indication of senility." Nona laughed and picked up her food. "We'll have Norma back from the roller-skating party in Le Mars by eleven tonight."

Irene turned serious. "I'm glad for my daughter that the church youth group is active again, Nona. You and Milly Brooks deserve a lot of credit for taking time to be the sponsors."

"Milly and I love it," Nona said.

"I'm happy that you do, but I'd think there are other things two young women could be doing on a Saturday night than taking a bunch of kids roller-skating," Irene said.

"Milly's fiancé is on a business trip this weekend and I don't have anyone pounding my door down. I can't think of anything I'd rather do than roller-skate," she said. But she thought of how she hadn't been on roller skates in years.

"I've got to move. Basketball practice at ten," she said. "See you."

"The thought has occurred to me that I can't remember when I skated last," Milly said.

She and Nona were standing in line behind the twenty members of the youth group, waiting to get skates. The rink was semidark, with spinning colored lights casting circles on the floor. Tables and chairs were arranged on a riser, which encompassed the rink.

"You must have been reading my mind," Nona said.

Milly, a little over five feet in height, was the school librarian. On workdays, she dressed like a fashion plate, her dark hair done in a sleek bun. Weekends she dressed "to fit the occasion," as she called it. Tonight, she wore stone-washed jeans and an oversize gray sweatshirt. A new perm gave her a rather wild and energetic look.

Milly pointed. "Look at those kids go! What if I crash? Do you think out school insurance will cover a broken arm?"

Nona gave Milly a gentle shove. "Gee, Milly. You do know how to instill confidence."

A few minutes later, the two were seated at a table and put on their skates. Three of their charges—William, Cara and Missy—eagerly led Milly down to the floor, with promises to be right back to do the same for Nona.

Gripping the back of her chair, Nona cautiously stood up and took a couple of small steps. "Okay!" she whispered gleefully.

No! Not okay! She started rolling slowly down the riser, which, she belatedly discovered, was built on a slight incline.

Brake! she thought. She toed down and staggered forward. She grabbed for something, knocked over a chair and rolled on, clutching a sweater she didn't own.

Now there was nothing between her and the floor. "Oh—" She was suddenly stopped by strong fingers clutching her under her arms, which triggered a quivering sensation in her stomach.

"Hello again, Nona Alexander," a familiar voice crooned in her ear.

Amid the exquisite feelings caused by Nicholas's "catch", Nona wondered if it was her destiny to have him witness some of her worst moments.

"Thank you for stopping me," she said. Either her voice was fluttering in her chest or her heart was.

He lowered his hands to her waist to steady her. "Glad I was—" she turned to look at him over her shoulder, and her cheek collided with his nose; apparently he'd leaned closer to speak "—here to stop you." He rubbed his nose while she rubbed her cheek. "You're a one-woman wrecking crew, aren't you?" he asked, chuckling.

"I haven't been on skates in a long time," Nona said.

"I never would have guessed."

"I knew you would never have guessed. That's why I told you." She'd sounded breathless because she was breathless. His touch had thrown her body chemistry out of kilter. She was tingling with warmth and she didn't know whether or not she could catch her next breath without gasping.

She might have done something really stupid like saying, I'm happy to see you again, except she noted two things simultaneously. Missy, Cara and William were making their way toward her, and a beautiful, dark-haired woman had moved into view and was openly studying her with more than casual interest.

He's married! Nona thought.

She quickly extracted herself from Kendrick's hands and rolled toward William, hoping he would react fast enough to catch her. He did, and she ended with her arms draped over his and Missy's shoulders. Smiling back at Nicholas, she tried to look as if she'd intended the pose.

"Thank you again, Mr. Kendrick," she called brightly. Missy and William untangled themselves from her, then faced the same direction she was. To them she murmured, "Get me out of here."

The girls were buzzing. "Isn't he the referee from last night?" Cara wanted to know.

"The *blind* one?" Missy asked.

"Yes. The blind one," Nona agreed.

"Gosh. He's good-looking. Don't you think so, Mrs. A.?" Cara added.

"Uh...yes. I suppose," Nona replied.

"What's he doing here?" Missy asked.

"I wouldn't have the vaguest." Nona suddenly remembered that in her right hand she still held a sweater. "Cara? See this?" She waggled it.

"Yes. I see it."

"It doesn't belong to me," Nona said.

"Whose is it?"

"It belongs to the table—" Nona indicated it with her head "—up there, where that woman wearing the blue blouse appears to be looking for something. I sort of caught the sweater when I grabbed for the chair."

"Give it to me," Cara said. "I'll go up and explain to the woman you didn't mean to heist it."

Oh, joy, Nona thought. What a night! Heisting a sweater, knocking chairs over—and a *married* Kendrick. But she wouldn't think about that right now. She was going to concentrate on skating.

After two swings around the huge floor with William bellowing, "Coming through! Watch out! Coming through!" Nona decided she had spent enough time in training.

When she spotted Milly just ahead, she announced, "I'm going to give it a try alone."

"You're doing okay," Milly said as Nona joined her. "Especially after your obtrusive beginning." Then she nudged Nona and gestured in Kendrick's direction.

He and his wife had been joined by a dark-haired little girl, obviously their daughter. He and the girl were putting on skates.

"The new minister is a good-looking man," Milly said. "But I don't suppose you noticed." She giggled.

"What new minister?"

"Nicholas Kendrick. I thought it was kind of gallant of him to keep you from falling on your tush."

Nicholas Kendrick a minister? "You must have him confused with somebody else. He's not a minister," Nona said. He looked up and caught her staring.

Milly smiled at Kendrick and waved. Nona's blush deepened. Then she noticed what she had been too embarrassed to notice earlier. He was wearing blue jeans and a green knit shirt, and it was clear that it wasn't the zebra stripes on his referee uniform that had given him broad shoulders. He was just plain built.

"He's a referee, Milly. Not a minister," Nona reiterated, sounding a bit panicked.

"If it's going to upset you, he isn't a minister," Milly said. "And the night you had basketball practice and I went to the reception the Oak Valley Ladies' Aid had for their new minister, Nicholas Kendrick wasn't the man I met. Okay? Feel better?"

How could she feel any worse? Nona wondered. She had told a minister she was going to go home and pray! But she could feel worse. He had to be Jon Sr. and Emily's minister.

"For heaven's sake," Nona said. "A minister!"

"He told me he'd be substituting for our conference—" Milly paused, her eyes growing wide. "He worked the game last night? He's the one who called the T on you?"

Milly was a team chaperone, but she'd missed the game because she'd attended a meeting of school librarians held in Sioux City. "The same," Nona said. "His wife is beautiful."

"Reverend Kendrick's wife, Corinne, died in a car accident six months ago. The woman is his sister, Ivy Kipling. She's a widow. That's her daughter, Kelly."

"Six months ago," Nona murmured. "It must be difficult for him. And now a new church so far from home."

"I gathered from what Ivy said that his wife was quite a help in his ministry. That was one of the reasons Ivy came to Iowa with him—to help him settle in the new parsonage, work with the women's groups, the kinds of things his wife did. Ivy plans on staying until next spring so Kelly's schooling won't be interrupted."

The thoughts Nona had been having about Nicholas hadn't been platonic. They hadn't even been the kind of thoughts she had ever had about other men. It beat all, fantasizing about a minister! She was mortified.

"You want a soda?" Milly asked. Nona shook her head. All she really wanted to do was fade into the colors on the floor. "See you later," Milly said, and glided off the floor.

After tying the laces on his roller skates, Nicholas stood. Kelly had already moved toward the floor. "Sure you don't want to try skating, Ivy?"

Ivy stuck a strand of dark hair back into her bun, then fussed with the black-and-white silk scarf pinned fashionably at her neck. "I'm too old for such foolishness, Nicholas."

"You're thirty-six, two years older than I am." He grinned. "Are you implying I'm being foolish?"

Ivy laughed. "The difference between us, dear brother, is that I intend to grow old gracefully. I don't think a broken leg would be especially graceful."

There had been a time in his sister's life when she would have been game to try anything. But since Bill's death four years ago, Ivy appeared more and more to be a spectator rather than a participant in life. He'd accepted her offer to come to Iowa with him hoping that a new environment would give her a new perspective on life, which was exactly what he had been wanting for himself when he had accepted the call to the Oak Valley church.

"This is going to be fun, Ivy," Nicholas offered.

"Another time, maybe."

Nicholas knew defeat when he faced it. He moved to the edge of the floor where Kelly was waiting.

"Ready to dance?" he asked, smiling down at his eight-year-old niece. He extended his hand.

"I want to skate with my friends right now," Kelly announced. "But I'll dance with you later."

"You're turning me down? I'm hurt," he said.

"You're teasing, Uncle Nicholas."

"Yes, I am. Have fun, sweetheart."

Kelly stepped onto the floor and skated away, weaving through the others. She turned back to him, smiled and waved.

His thoughts flashed to Corinne. How could she have not wanted children? He had married her not because he had great passion for her but because he had believed he loved her and that she loved him. At first their marriage had been serene, uneventful, with the exception of their disagreement over having children.

Was it when she'd refused to have a child that their marriage had started to go wrong? The question ate at him. Should he have suspected then that behind her sweetness was a neurotic need to be the center of his universe?

Nicholas stepped to the floor. As he skated, he spoke to members of his youth group and smiled a greeting to the young people he didn't know, all the while telling himself that he did *not* have an objective in mind.

But he could see Nona just ahead. He smiled. He hadn't intended to catch her the intimate way he had, but in those fleeting seconds his fingers had memorized the soft contour of her breasts beneath the red jersey she was wearing, and the smell of her perfume. He'd been blissfully light-headed right up to the point when her cheek smacked his nose.

She had gotten her skates somewhat under control. Her long jean-covered legs were moving more or less rhythmically. He couldn't see her face, but he knew she was smiling because the three youngsters she was with had laughed at something she'd said before moving on.

"I'm surprised to see you here," he said once he was beside her.

Nona's precarious balance depended on keeping her eyes straight ahead. That definitely meant *not* meeting his gaze.

"Why should my being here surprise you?" she asked stiffly.

"I thought you'd still be home praying," he replied.

"Implying I should be home praying. Aren't you being sacrilegious?" she asked.

An inadvertent glance at him nearly cost her her balance. Chuckling, he slipped his arm around her waist to steady her. Again his touch triggered warmth and a lovely feeling of mellowness that her body absorbed like a dry sponge.

After he released her, she wondered how anything that could feel so deliciously good could be wrong. But it *was* wrong. He was a minister! Every minister's wife Nona had ever known devoted all of her time to church activities. Her marriage had failed because she hadn't had time to devote to Jon's professional needs. He was a real estate agent and a part of selling was wining and dining clients. It had reached the point where Nona had felt that she had no time to herself.

Suddenly Nona decided that whatever she was feeling for Nicholas was all right as long as he didn't know about it. After all, they weren't planning a future together, just getting acquainted.

"I gather Milly Brooks told you I'm the new minister at Oak Valley."

Nona fought her awareness of him by telling herself it was a one-sided attraction. He was interested in her only because she reminded him of someone. But how in the dickens did one act in the presence of a minister whose maleness emanated so strongly?

"That's right, Reverend Kendrick. I wish I'd known it last night."

"You were calling me Nicholas. I wish you'd continue to do it. What difference would my being a minister have made? Your player was charging."

Nona glanced up and lost her balance again. He grabbed her and drew her into his arms.

They stood in the middle of the floor, with skaters going around them. Nona saw only Nicholas, felt her length very lightly but securely pressed to his—then she remembered he was a minister who was a recent widower. She was a divorcée. Bad combination.

"Okay now?" Nicholas asked, sounding concerned.

"Okay," she said. When he released her, she skated ahead. "I still don't agree that Kate charges," she added.

"Let's find a quiet spot and discuss it," he suggested.

Nona had a no forming on her lips, but he didn't give her a chance to verbalize it. He guided her from the floor to a table, helped her sit, then drew a chair close and eased down on it.

"Now, back to Kate," he said. "The girl is a terrific natural talent but when she delivers her jump shot, ninety percent of the time she's leaning into her guard."

"Kate has a right to come down, doesn't she?"

"She had a right to come down, but not on her opponent's head. If you don't mind a suggestion, in practice sessions, try putting a chair in the position of the guard and make Kate shoot against it. She'll learn to jump straight up and down."

"I can visualize what you're suggesting. I'll try it and see what happens."

"You mean you're going to accept my advice just like that? With no argument?" He seemed surprised.

"Yes."

"Come on. Let's debate it."

"It sounds like a reasonable suggestion to me," Nona said slowly. "Why should I debate it with you?"

"Because I enjoy the sound of your voice and the sparkle in your eyes when you're emotionally involved." He propped an elbow on the table and rested his cheek on his hand.

He was teasing, of course, Nona knew. But she was reading suggestions in his eyes, in the way he leaned toward her and looked so attentive. She forced herself back to reality. The kind of woman he would truly be interested in would be the kind his wife had been. Quite a help in his ministry, according to Milly.

"I am usually in control of my emotions," she stated, managing to keep the surge of reaction to him from leaking out in her voice. "In spite of what you saw last night."

"Your girls were outclassed last night," he said. When Nona pursed her lips to protest, he added quickly "But not outplayed or out-hustled. You thought Kate needed defending, so you defended her."

"Which was not very bright of me, right?" she asked.

"Not very bright," he agreed. "But understandable. And perhaps even justified."

Nona sighed. Her thoughts flew to Jon. She had never been angry with him. Hurt and disappointed, yes. But never stomach-cramping angry, which was how she'd felt last night.

"It may have been understandable, but in my opinion, extreme anger is rarely justified," she said. He ran his fingers through his dark hair. It was silky and shiny, she noted. His eyes sparkled mischievously.

"I know you're laughing at me," she asserted. "But in spite of what you're thinking, I did lose a good deal of sleep worrying about what I'd done and wondering what kind of impression it left with my girls."

I'm lying to a minister! she thought. The sleep she'd lost was because she couldn't stop thinking about him. Wondering if he was married. Wondering if she would see him again. Hoping she would.

Chapter Three

"I know being a role model isn't easy," Nicholas said. "But I believe there are times when it's better to express extreme anger rather than control it."

"And I know you're trying to ease my guilt," Nona said. "But you know and I know there were other ways I could have stated my case without losing my temper and goading you into an argument."

"Do you believe I'm above losing my temper just because I'm a minister?"

"What I believe is that because you're a minister you've learned to control your temper."

"In part you're right. A minister is expected to be above displays of name-calling and kicking things," he said slowly, enjoying the marvelous animation in her eyes as she reacted to his words. "But I'm guilty of being short-tempered and when I get mad, rather than show it, I sulk."

He noted the inviting trembling of her lower lip and knew she was keeping herself from laughing. "Tell me about yourself, Nona Alexander," he said.

Nona wanted to. She wanted to tell him not about the mundane stuff in her life, but about the fiber, what made her tick. She'd like to say what a failure she had been as a businessman's wife so he'd know she wouldn't make a good wife for a minister. But since they'd just met, he'd probably think she was crazy if she did express all that. So she decided to just think it and to think she was crazy to be thinking it.

"I'm doing what I always wanted to do—teach. I taught four years in Sioux Falls. After—" She paused. "I'm divorced. I suppose Arlo told you?"

"Arlo said Jon was tall, blond and brilliant," Nicholas said.

"Jon was all those things. After our divorce I taught in Sioux Falls another year," she said. She shifted in her chair, and her roller skate shot out and banged his foot. He smiled. She continued as if nothing had happened. "When the teaching position in the English department opened up in Beaver Crossing, I jumped at the chance. I live with my mother."

"Ah, yes," Nicholas said. "The gray-haired lady with the marvelous smile. Jenny Niles."

"Arlo again?" Nona asked. He nodded. She liked the feeling of knowing he cared enough to be interested. "I can see by the way you're grinning that Mother was up to something last night. What did she do?"

"She kept winking at me," Nicholas said. "At first I thought it was a tic. When I realized it wasn't, I winked back."

"She's harmless...I think. But you encouraged her by winking back?"

Nicholas loved the way there was always a smile lurking on Nona's lips and in her eyes. He didn't know why he was attracted to her, besides the obvious male-female thing, but he liked how she made him feel—an optimistic twenty-year-old again.

"I always wink at special people," he said, winking.

Nona recoiled. It was hardly a tease, but it rocked her. She felt herself growing weak. I've never met a minister like him, she thought. All right, I've never met a man like him.

"Mother *is* a special person," she agreed. She was giving herself a mental pat for speaking sanely, when she found herself blurting, "Did you just wink at me?"

"I told you I always do at special people," Nicholas said. He winked. "There it goes again."

Nona fought to control a giggle. "It's a good thing you're a good judge of character, or you could get yourself in trouble."

"With you and your mother, it wasn't difficult," he said. "You have special written all over you. It shows in your smiles. You enjoy life."

An aura of intimacy surrounded them. Nona found it too difficult to deal with, so she looked at the floor and waved to William, Cara and Missy.

After a moment, she forced her gaze back to Nicholas. "Mother has rheumatoid arthritis, but she doesn't give in. Thank goodness most of the time the arthritis is under control and she's able to get around."

"Did you come back to Beaver Crossing because you thought you could help your mother out?"

"I really wish I could say my motivation was so noble," Nona said. "But that wasn't the reason."

"What was?"

Nona half smiled. Only a moment ago, she'd decided not to reveal anything of a personal nature about herself, but how could she resist a man with a wicked wink and a knack of asking questions that probed beneath the surface.

"The old story," she said. "I'm sure you've heard it countless times. After the divorce, I was feeling rotten about myself—the shattered self-esteem syndrome. So I came home because my mother is the kind of person who wouldn't allow me to feel sorry for myself."

"Since my wife's death, I've been going through the shattered self-esteem syndrome myself," Nicholas found himself confessing. He had thought he would never admit it to anyone. "Maybe self-pity does have something to do with it."

His reference to the loss of his wife caught Nona off guard. She didn't know what she was feeling. Sympathy, certainly. And jealousy. Because his marriage had been good, when hers hadn't been? Or because the hazel eyes gazing at her now had looked upon another woman with love, the kind that Jon had never had for her. She didn't know.

THE PERFECT WIFE

She was about to extend her condolences when a woman's voice asked, "Nicholas?"

Nona looked up to discover Ivy approaching the table. The older woman was smiling, but her smile didn't seem to reach her hazel eyes. She was starchy, the opposite of her brother.

"Ivy, join us," Nicholas said. He stood, pulled out the chair next to him and made the introductions.

After Ivy had sat down, Nona extended her hand. Ivy's grasp was firm, a bit of a surprise to her. "Hello, Ivy," she said.

"Pleased to meet you, Nona," Ivy said. She folded her hands on her lap. "I was visiting with Mrs. Timmons. She told me you're a basketball coach. That must be very interesting."

Who was Mrs. Timmons? Nona wondered, then remembered. Agnes Brent Timmons had gone to school with her mother. She glanced around. At a table across the rink, a heavyset woman was looking their way, waving. Sure enough, that was Agnes. Nona waved back.

Nona would have described coaching as a lot of things besides interesting, but it was obvious Ivy was only making conversation. "Yes," she said. "I find coaching interesting."

Nicholas leaned back out of Ivy's sight. Grinning, he made a "T" with his hands—the signal for a technical. Nona coughed, trying to cover a laugh.

"I think at one time Nicholas thought about coaching," Ivy said, turning to look at him. "Didn't you?"

Nicholas's hands were now lying innocently on the table and his expression was free of guile. "That's a fact, Ivy," he said.

"Did you know Nona is married to Jon, Sr. and Emily Alexander's son?" Ivy asked. She smiled at Nona.

Nona felt the bottom fall out of her stomach. She knew Nicholas had probably already guessed who the Alexanders were, but the abruptness of Ivy's announcement left her searching for words.

Nona said, "The Alexanders are lovely people," while Nicholas said, "I'd guessed that Ivy."

"But they are my *ex*-in-laws. Jon and I are divorced," Nona added lamely.

Ivy's eyes widened. Her fingers flew to her mouth. "I'm sorry, Nona. I didn't know. Mrs. Timmons didn't tell me."

"You didn't offend me, Ivy."

"I talk too much," Ivy said. Her hands fluttered in the air nervously. "I always have, but I seem to be worse since my husband died. Bill would give me the eye when I started to rattle on." She chuckled, but her chuckle turned into a strangled sob. She wiped away a tear with a finger.

Nona touched Ivy's hand. "I know how difficult it is for you, especially with Kelly. My father died when I was twelve, and Mother went through some difficult years raising five children alone."

Ivy smiled weakly. "Thank you. You're kind. And I'm just a weeper. Bill's been dead four years...so I should be able to talk about him...remember the good times, you know."

"I do understand," Nona said.

"I was doing rather well adjusting to Bill's death until Corinne was killed," Ivy said, dabbing her eyes. "Then it all came rushing back. Corinne was a dear person. And a perfect helpmate for Nicholas, wasn't she?" Ivy asked, turning to her brother.

Nicholas cringed inside. All Ivy knew about his marriage was what Corinne had told her, and what she had seen. On the surface, their marriage had appeared perfect. None of Corinne's jealous tirades, none of his stoic withdrawal had been on display. Both of them had kept up appearances for the sake of his ministry.

He cleared his throat and narrowed his eyes slightly, trying to send Ivy the message to drop the subject. She was making Nona nervous—and making a wreck out of him.

"In many respects Corinne was a help," he said truthfully, knowing his tension sounded in his voice.

"Corinne had her master's degree in education," Ivy said, focusing her attention on Nona. "But she felt her obligations to Nicholas's congregation came first so she never taught."

Nicholas tried to get a word in, but Ivy prattled on. Corinne hadn't taught because she didn't want to teach.

"Did you find it difficult to juggle two careers, Nona?" Ivy asked.

Nona glanced furtively at Nicholas, who was grim-faced, before turning back to Ivy, who was totally oblivious to the tension she had created by talking about Corinne. Just as obvious was Ivy's not getting the silent message Nicholas had sent her—he didn't want to discuss Corinne.

"Frankly, I didn't do a good job of juggling two careers," she admitted. She prayed for wings. All she wanted to do was fly away. "It takes a lot of energy...uh...having two careers," she added inanely.

"Corinne had a lot of energy," Ivy said enthusiastically. "She was a tall woman." Suddenly she stopped talking and stared at Nona.

Nona felt Nicholas's gaze on her. She looked at him and discovered he was studying her as intensely as he had last night when he had thought he knew her. Corinne, she thought. Somehow, she reminded both Nicholas and Ivy of his wife.

And now Nicholas was drawing comparisons between her, the busy career woman with the short temper who'd been a flop at juggling two careers, and his wife who had given up teaching to devote herself to marriage and his ministry. The longer Nona stayed where she was, the worse she would look in comparison.

She knew it was a matter of pride, but she couldn't bear his silent scrutiny any longer. She said quickly, "I've enjoyed visiting with you. But I believe I'm going to try my luck at skating again. Nice to have met you, Ivy. Good luck with your ministry, Nicholas."

She stood and without a backward glance rolled toward the floor.

Nicholas knew she was fleeing from Ivy's well-intended but misguided chatter. Too often Ivy talked about Corinne. And he allowed his sister to keep her illusions. After all, what good could come from maligning Corinne?

"I'm going to skate. Do you mind?" he asked abruptly.

"Of course not." Ivy's gaze went to Kelly, who was laughing. "I think Kelly's missed having you take her skating every Saturday afternoon," she said.

Nicholas stood. "You're missing something, too. You should give skating a fling."

Ivy laughed. Nicholas smiled, then went to the edge of the rink to wait for Nona. When she passed by, he stepped onto the floor and joined her.

"You were running from me," he said.

"I wasn't running."

She didn't glance at him but kept moving forward. All right, he thought, don't look. "I saw that Ivy made you nervous. She tends to rattle, and after she made the gaffe about Jon, Sr. and Emily, her embarrassment caused her to forget to put a lid on it."

"I understood what had happened to her. But I thought you were the one who looked uneasy," Nona said.

"I was uneasy." Nicholas had to do a quick side step to avoid crashing into a pair who were dancing. "This is impossible. We can't talk while we're skating," he said. He took Nona's hand and guided her from the floor.

Nona wasn't sure their conversation wasn't over. But rather than create a scene, she allowed him to lead her to a nearby table.

The moment they sat down, she said, "I remind you of your wife, don't I?"

Nicholas reflected that comparing Nona and Corinne was like comparing day and night. Corinne was stalked by fears that tormented her all the time. Nona was like the sun and showed it in her glowing smiles.

"There's nothing about you that reminds me of Corinne," Nicholas said. Suddenly he wished for the music to go down and for the twirling lights to turn off. He wanted Nona to concentrate on what he was saying, without distraction. "But I did have an uncanny feeling I'd met you before."

Nona studied his expression, searching for a hint of dishonesty. She saw nothing but openness. Still, she didn't believe him. "I didn't have the chance to express my sympathy. I am very sorry about your wife's death."

Nicholas sighed deeply. He was sorry, too. Pained. There was so much he wanted to tell her. How his grief was grounded in guilt. How Corinne's death had made him search for the truth about himself. How he needed to know what kind of man he was. How he'd started to think he might find the answer since last night when she'd turned and looked at him.

"Grieving is a difficult process," he said. "Especially when you know in your heart there were things you should have done and didn't do. Things you said and shouldn't have said."

She clasped her hands on the table. "I think it's that way with everyone when they lose someone they love."

"That's true. But before this conversation goes any further, we need to get something straight," Nicholas said forcefully. "You bear no resemblance to anyone I know or have ever known."

He placed his hands over hers. The contact sent shock waves through his body. He quickly removed his hand. "So that leaves other possibilities to consider," he said. "Destiny. Fate."

Nona recovered from the pleasing feel of his touch in time to see the flicker of humor in his eyes. "Now, that does sound like a line," she teased gently.

"No line."

"Then it's pretty heavy stuff—destiny, fate."

He grinned. "I think so, too, so I'm settling on good fortune. It was my good fortune to meet you."

"Or happenstance," Nona offered. "It could have been happenstance. Arlo's partner happened to get sick. You happened to be the substitute official called for the Cranston game. And I happened to be coaching the Beaver Crossing girls."

"It wasn't happenstance." He laughed. Then in a more serious voice, he asked, "Would you have dinner with me?"

She was taken off guard by the quick change in his emotion. Laughing one moment to quietly impassioned the next. "I—I" she stammered.

Just then, William skated up. "Hey, hey, hey, Mrs. A., what have we got going on here?" he asked lightheartedly.

"William! Move along," Nona retorted, waving him away. She watched him rejoin Cara and Missy.

Nona chuckled, but the incident was a reminder of why she shouldn't have dinner with Nicholas. If she were to go out with him, their relationship would be subject for speculation. She didn't want to be responsible in any way for undermining his position with his congregation.

"I don't think dinner would be a good idea," she said.

"You're dating someone special," Nicholas said.

"There is no one special," she said. She paused, then asked, "You haven't lived in a small town before, have you?"

"As a matter of fact, I was born and raised in Houston. My first church was in Dallas. Don't tell me those stories I'd heard about finding serenity in small towns were propaganda."

Nona smiled. "Serenity you'll find."

"Good."

"You will also find that a small town and the surrounding area is like one family."

"I'd heard that, too. Sounds good to me."

"Nicholas," she said, then suddenly thought of how she could lose herself in his gaze. "You will also find that nothing goes on in this entire county without someone knowing someone who knows about it. Get the idea?"

"Sure, I get the idea," Nicholas said. "But I don't get the point."

"Ninety-nine percent of the population would think it was great that the teacher and the minister were dating. But one percent would whisper, 'Have you heard the minister's going with the divorcée?'"

He considered what she'd said for a moment. "You're worried about appearances?" he asked.

"That pretty much says it," Nona agreed.

He leaned forward, intent but smiling. "I've learned through personal experience that you can't always trust appearances."

Nona felt herself weakening. What harm would there be in going out with him if he didn't care how it appeared to other people?

"Uncle Nicholas! Uncle Nicholas!" Kelly skated up. She bobbed her head at Nona, saying, "Hello," then turned to Nicholas and asked, "Please dance with me?"

"Excuse me, Nona," Nicholas said. "My best girl is asking me to dance."

"Then you're excused."

Nicholas stood and smiled down at her. "Don't go away. I'll be back."

He took Kelly's hand and they moved into the flow of skaters. They spun. Kelly dipped gracefully, her laugh rippling across the rink. They had practiced often, Nona decided because they really were dancing.

With Ivy's husband dead and Nicholas's not having children of his own, Nicholas probably was like a second father to Kelly. And it was easy to see he enjoyed playing that role.

"I declare," Milly said as she pulled up. "I love it. I love it. I love it."

"Nicholas and Kelly are really something, aren't they?" Nona asked.

"I hate a kid who can skate like that," Milly observed, her smile belying her statement. "But what I was talking about was you and Nicholas. Mrs. Timmons is right—you and he look fabulous together."

"Mrs. Timmons?"

"I was visiting with her, which you might have noticed had your attention not been on somebody else. She said the ladies in Nicholas's congregation had been wondering who they could line up for him. She's positively giggly over the prospect of a romance blossoming between you and him."

"Milly! How could you gossip about us?" Nona asked more sharply than she'd intended.

Milly looked hurt. "Mrs. Timmons wasn't gossiping. And neither was I. You know me better than that."

"I'm sorry," Nona apologized. "I didn't mean to sound harsh. But there's no chance of a romance. It's silly to even talk about it."

Milly's cheerfulness returned immediately. "Don't tell me he's going to be just a friend?"

"If he's going to be anything, it will be just a friend," Nona asserted.

Milly groaned. "You've got more darned men friends than you need, Nona. What you need is a hot-blooded lover."

Nicholas and Kelly danced past, two-stepping in perfect beat with the music. Nicholas's smile at Kelly's upturned face was beautiful, Nona was thinking when his gaze came to her.

Milly cleared her throat. "And there he is," she observed. "The perfect candidate."

"Don't joke about it," Nona said.

"Who's joking?" Milly asked nonchalantly, then skated away.

Nicholas came back. Nona wished she had had the foresight to vanish before he returned because she knew from the expression on his face that he intended to pick up right where he'd left off.

"Before we were distracted," he said, "I'd asked you to dinner."

"I'd rather not," Nona said.

"Are you turning me down because you're indifferent or because you're afraid people will talk?" he asked.

His expression told her he *wasn't* indifferent to her, and he was asking her to be honest enough to admit she wasn't indifferent to him.

She looked away and saw Milly skating with Cara. Milly arched her brows at her and smiled knowingly. "Mrs. Timmons and my friend Milly already see romance in the air for us," she said.

Nicholas laughed. "I'll admit they're getting a little ahead of themselves... or we aren't keeping up."

Nona ignored his suggestive comment even though her heart's beating speeded. "I'd say they're getting a lot ahead of themselves. But that's how rumors start."

"Don't take it so seriously, Nona," he said winningly. "Mrs. Timmons has been plotting the demise of my bachelor status ever since I arrived. If she hadn't picked you, she would have picked somebody else. I'm happy with the call she made."

Nona was quivering in places she'd never quivered, and felt anticipation as she'd never felt it before. Dangerous stuff. She straightened on the chair.

"I enjoy your company, Nicholas, but I don't think dinner would be a good idea." Trying hard to hide her disappointment, she added brightly, "I'll look forward to seeing you when you're called on to referee again. And I'm going to take your advice with Kate. We'll see what develops."

"All right," Nicholas agreed. "We'll see what develops."

Chapter Four

Nona was singing when she walked into the kitchen at eleven that night. "Hello, Tomkins," she warbled to the orange tomcat who stood waiting to be let out. She held the door open for him.

"Hi, Nona," Jenny singsonged from the front room. "Would you please put Tomkins out?"

"Already did," Nona said. She went to her mother, kissed her cheek, then collapsed on the davenport. "My heels have blisters."

"Blisters are a cause to rejoice?" Jenny closed her book and laid it on her lap.

Nona rested her elbows on her knees and her chin in her palms. She'd been thinking of Nicholas, and a wonderful feeling of lightness had hummed through her body. "Do I sound as if I'm rejoicing?" she asked.

"You came in the house singing and you ask me if you're happy? Come here and let me smell your breath. I think you must have been drinking."

"Nicholas Kendrick was at the skating party," Nona said.

"Now I understand," Jenny said.

Nona smiled. Nicholas had not pursued her after she'd stated her position, but she'd caught him looking at her each time she glanced in his direction. Which had been often, she had to admit. "We visited for a while."

"Then what?"

"I met his sister, Ivy, and his niece, Kelly. Kelly is eight. A bright and delightful child. You should see her skate," Nona said. "She even tried to teach me to dance on roller skates."

"What kind of luck did she have?"

"Let's just say I provided some free entertainment." Nona reclined and closed her eyes. "Nicholas is the new minister at Oak Valley," she added.

"I'd never have guessed! They never made ministers who looked like he does when I was growing up," Jenny commented.

Nona sat up. "My sentiment exactly. He's a widower. His wife was killed in a car accident six months ago." She paused. "He'd be about the same age you were when Dad died."

"When it happens so quickly to someone so young, a person questions why," Jenny said softly. "I know I did. And I imagine it would be as difficult for a minister as for any of us."

"I gather from what he told me he has moments of questioning why and feeling self-pity," Nona said. "Ivy's a widow, so she's sympathetic to what Nicholas is going through. From what I saw tonight, no matter how busy Nicholas is, he'd be lonely without Kelly and Ivy."

"I can understand that," Jenny said reflectively. "You try to keep busy, to keep from thinking about your loss. But every once in a while it sneaks up on you. I yearned to have your father around...just to talk to. I wanted to ask him, 'Should we put Lillian in braces? Should we make Ken take trumpet lessons?'" She chuckled. "Small problems, but that's when I was most lonely for your father, when I needed someone to bounce ideas around with. And no one seemed to fill the bill quite like he did."

Nona smiled. "I think it was that kind of loneliness for his wife that made Nicholas invite me to dinner."

"Really? When do you plan to go?"

"I didn't accept."

"Am I missing something?" Jenny asked.

Nona shook her head. "You never miss a thing, Mother. He's very attractive. Someone would talk."

"Any more talk than when you go out with Dave Herman?"

"Dave's a friend."

"He's a minister, too."

"He treats me like a sister."

"Because you treat him like your two brothers," Jenny pointed out smugly.

"Only you could take something illogical and make it sound logical. Dave needs a woman who would be a partner in his ministry. He doesn't consider me a prospect," Nona said emphatically. "Dave knows what a failure I was as a businessman's wife. The wife of a minister would have even more demands made on her time."

"I would hardly call you a failure as Jon's helpmate," Jenny grumbled. "It would have strained my patience if your father had expected me to entertain his friends and business acquaintances every weekend."

Nona smiled. "Thank you for the kind words, Mother, but your opinion is hardly objective. Granted, Jon had his shortcomings, but so did I."

Jenny leaned back, a dour expression on her face. "He was never interested in what you were doing. Why do you defend him?"

Nona sometimes wondered herself. "I defend him because he was the man I married," she said. "He always wanted me to quit teaching. Who knows what would have happened if I'd done it?"

"Do you really believe that would have stopped his—to be polite, I'll say outside interest?" Jenny tapped her fingers on the book.

"He told me Joann was the only one he'd been involved with."

"One transgression was not what ruined your marriage. Jon lacked emotional maturity," Jenny said. "He wanted you to take care of him just as his mother had. And rather than demanding he be independent, you mothered him because you've been mothering people all of your life, beginning with your brothers and sisters."

"Call Nicholas Kendrick and tell him you've changed your mind about dinner."

"I don't know—"

"I understand your reluctance. The man is as blind as a bat," Jenny said, adding, "but he's a wicked winker!"

Oh, yes, Nona thought, he was a wicked winker. And he had made her feel he cared about her in a special way. She sighed. "I'd be asking for heartbreak, Mother."

"Or happiness."

"I hate to dampen such optimism, but last night he told me he thought he knew me. I think I remind him of his wife."

Jenny pressed her lips together thoughtfully. "Is that so bad?"

"I don't want to be anybody's second love ever again." Nona stood. "I'm going to bed. Anything I can do for you before I go upstairs?"

"Yes."

"Name it."

"Get happy again."

Nona kissed her mother's cheek. "I'm happy. I really am."

She was happy, she told herself. This feeling that she was going to miss something by not allowing herself to get to know Nicholas would pass quickly. Though she would wonder for a while what might have happened between them had circumstances been different.

* * *

When Nicholas heard the back door of the church open and shut, he swiveled his chair toward the study door wondering who'd come in. A moment later, Kelly, wearing her coat, knitted hat and mittens, appeared in the doorway.

Kelly had never seen snow, and each day since the beginning of winter, she had looked for it. So far she'd been disappointed. "You look like you're on your way to build a snowman," he said.

"There's no snow, Uncle Nicholas," she said, giggling.

"I forgot that a person has to have snow to build a snowman," he said as she walked to him.

"No, you didn't. You're teasing."

"So what are you up to?"

"Mama and me are going to get groceries. What are you doing Uncle Nicholas? Still working on a sermon?"

That was what he'd told Kelly when he had left the house to walk across the lawn to the church, two hours ago. And that had been his intent, but he hadn't worked on his sermon long before he set it aside to take out a sketch pad.

He drew to relax, and whenever he was dealing with a difficult problem. Over the last two weeks he had often reached for the sketch pad—and Nona's face kept appearing on the paper.

"I was working on a sermon. I'm not right now. What do you want, kiddo?"

Kelly studied the pencil drawing. "Mama said I had to ask you—I know her!" she said. "I skated with her and taught her to dance. She's nice. She told me her name but I forgot it."

"Her name is Nona," Nicholas said. "She's a teacher."

Kelly leaned closer and pointed to the girl in the picture. "I know her, too."

Nicholas had sketched Nona comforting one of her players. He thought the girl's name was Cara. "You do?"

"Sure. She was at the roller-skating party."

He nodded, though he couldn't remember whether or not Cara had. Once he had seen Nona, his focus had been only on her, and the others had faded into the background. "What did you have to ask me?"

"I want Mama to buy pizza," Kelly said, her eyes bright and hopeful. "But Mama said she didn't know. We had pizza last week, so it would be up to you. Can we get a pizza, Uncle Nicholas?"

"I love pizza," Nicholas said. "I could eat it every night of the week."

Kelly's smile widened. She danced out into the hall, singing, "I knew it! I knew it! We're going to have pizza!"

Laughing, Nicholas leaned back in the chair. He marveled at her exuberance—the childlike attitude that all one had to do to be granted a favor was ask—and wondered what happened to it when one grew up.

He wanted to call Nona and ask her to share an evening with him. He yearned to be granted this favor, but he had lost that youthful sureness that his wish would be fulfilled. Now he feared rebuke and censure.

When the memory of the night Corinne died started to work its way to the surface, Nicholas walked to the window and looked out, willing it away. But the memory came flooding back—the harsh words, his futile threat to walk out unless they sought marriage counseling and Corinne's storming out of the house and driving off.

Nicholas shuddered and walked back to his chair. He looked down on the sketch of Nona's face. There was something about her that reached out to him. And he wanted to reach back.

But did he have the right? He hadn't lived up to the expectations Corinne had of him, and the expectations he'd had of himself. He'd contributed to the unhappiness of one woman. Perhaps had driven her to her death...

What made him think he could make Nona happy?

But even as he thought that, he felt joy. He'd been called to referee a game with Arlo tonight at Beaver Crossing. He was going to see Nona. And he couldn't quell the excitement he experienced at the prospect.

Nona and Mel stood on the sidelines watching the girls warm up. Nona had the game ball and was occasionally bouncing it.

"The girls look sharp tonight," Mel said.

"What? You don't need the weekend to think it over?" Nona quipped.

"That trick with the chair seemed to work for Kate," Mel said.

"Seems like."

"We'll see tonight for sure," Mel offered. "Superintendent Krammer just told me Kendrick will be working the game with Arlo."

Nona's heart flipped. Her gaze flew to Arlo. The basketball fell from her hand and rolled toward the bleachers. "Really," she said.

Mel watched the ball roll, making the point that he'd seen the effect his announcement had on her. "I heard he saved you from falling on your duff at the roller-skating party," he observed.

Nona turned to him, frowning. "Milly has a big mouth."

"Milly didn't tell me. Grace did."

"How did your wife hear about it?"

"Her cousin is married to Agnes Timmons's brother."

Nona groaned.

"Take heart, Nona. I told Grace not to tell a soul, and swore her to it," he said, then snickered. "That's one rumor nipped in the bud."

"Good grief. And I haven't even gone out with the man," Nona said.

"It's only a matter of time, isn't it?" Mel smiled broadly.

"I think I hear someone calling you," Nona said. "Maybe it's your nurse."

"Oh, my, my, my. Touchy on the subject aren't we?" Mel strolled away, laughing.

Nona blushed. How much time did she have to compose herself? She hadn't expected to see Nicholas! Suddenly she felt worried about what she was wearing—her brown slack suit. A pretty brown, she thought.

The band tuned up. Nona gave instructions to her girls. Then she got the feeling...

Nicholas stepped into the gymnasium with Arlo and saw Nona—dressed in a doe-brown tailored slack suit with a blouse of darker brown. She was the magnet. He was the steel fragment being drawn to her. A clichéd description, but there wasn't anything that said it better.

Nothing could have stopped him from going to her.

The smile she offered when she turned and saw him coming, lifted him from the floor. He was buoyant, free of cares.

"I've got a lock on my temper tonight," she advised him once he stood before her.

"How did Kate come out against the chair?" he asked. He'd remembered the sound of her voice, the way she tilted her head as she listened attentively, and the creaminess of her complexion.

"I can't tell you that," Nona said cheerfully. Good grief! She had prepared for this moment by telling herself that she was *not* weak-willed like Jon. Physical attraction could be controlled. She couldn't remember what else she'd told herself. His presence muddled her thinking.

"You can't tell me? Why not?"

"Because if I were to tell the referee that in my opinion Kate no longer charges, it could be misconstrued by the opponents as trying to influence the outcome of the game."

Nicholas laughed. "And you'd never try to influence the ref, would you?"

Normally not, Nona thought. But you are an exception. "Of course not," she said, "but you'll see a vast improvement in the way Kate delivers her shot. Missy Wayman is my captain tonight."

Nona called Missy over, introduced her to Nicholas, then wandered away. Seeing Nicholas hadn't been so bad, she decided. In fact it had been rather pleasant. Rather pleasant? She was thrilled. Delighted. And from the way he had smiled at her, she had gathered he was pleased to see her.

But that was exactly the kind of fanciful thinking she couldn't indulge in. Nicholas Kendrick bestowed smiles on everyone. She glanced to where he was talking with Missy and saw him smiling at the girl, then at the Milford team captain. See, she told herself. She didn't stand out in the crowd. He was a smiler because he liked people.

But darn it, his smile was dynamite. She doubted if he meant to do it, but when he smiled at her, he became plain, unadulterated sexy. And she became plain unglued.

When the final whistle blew, Nicholas set the game ball near the scorers' table. He looked for Nona and saw she'd gone, so he followed Arlo into the hall leading to the locker rooms.

"There's Nona," Arlo said. "Nona!" he called. "Hold up."

Nona turned from the girls' locker-room door and walked toward them.

"I wanted to compliment you on the way you stayed in the coaching box tonight," Arlo told her drolly. "Quite an improvement over the Cranston game."

Other faces faded into nothingness for Nicholas again. Nona's smile, her laugh—he saw and heard those. And when the scent of her perfume drifted to his nostrils, he no longer smelled the heat of bodies in the closed area, but springtime freshness, dew on the grass and lilacs.

Nona wasn't looking at him. He didn't speak, but he wanted to tell her how even though he had just refereed a basketball game, he wouldn't have known that Beaver Crossing won the game if the score hadn't been on the scoreboard for him to see. All he remembered was watching her and wondering if he should ask to see her again, and if he'd be justified in asking.

Nona said cheerfully, "Not one technical tonight, Arlo. How about that?"

She was hiding the fluttering of her heart, the desire to touch Nicholas behind humor. She looked from Arlo to Nicholas and found his gaze on her.

She had just coached a basketball game, and she knew her girls won, but she couldn't remember the score. Her attention was focused on him. Whenever he looked at her, his look penetrated. It was as if against her will her soul was on display for him.

"And only one charge on Kate," she added. "Thank you for the tip about the folding chair, Nicholas."

"Folding chair?" Arlo asked.

Nona quickly explained, and Arlo laughed. They went on to talk about the conference standings. Then she said, "The girls are waiting for me. I have to go."

"Good visiting with you," Arlo said.

"Yes," Nicholas said. "Good visiting with you, Nona."

Nona took one last look into Nicholas's eyes and thought of how it could be weeks before she saw him again. "You, too," she said. "Now make sure the boys' basketball coaches stay in the coaching boxes."

"Men coaches," Arlo chided, "are more reasonable than female ones."

Nona laughed, then hurried down the hall. What had she wanted Nicholas to do? Offer another invitation so she could turn him down? Or offer her another invitation so she could accept?

She was tormented by a yearning she didn't understand, and was aching in ways she didn't want to acknowledge. Had she been less knowledgeable, she might have called what she was feeling infatuation.

But infatuation was a far cry from what she was feeling. It was her mind and soul that yearned for Nicholas and for the kind of love she had been denied.

She wished she had never met Nicholas Kendrick. Her life had been uncomplicated, peaceful—but it also had been without the pulsating joy just seeing Nicholas made her feel.

"Darn it," she muttered.

She put a broad smile on to cover her frustration, shoved open the locker-room door and called, "Way to go, girls!"

* * *

Nicholas followed Arlo to the lunchroom. They bought sodas and sat down. Arlo talked. Nicholas listened, but he was thinking about what had just happened in the hall.

In spite of the light conversation and the way the crowd had jostled them, he had known Nona was feeling as unsure and vulnerable as he.

She could be hurt. Had he learned enough from his past mistakes to avoid hurting her? Or would the guilt of knowing he'd failed Corinne when she'd needed him the most, always stalk his relationship with Nona?

Chapter Five

Nona, dressed for skiing, opened the basement door and went down the steps. With the first snow a week ago, she had carried her skis from the garage into the basement, and in spare moments, she had polished them in anticipation of her first cross-country ski trip.

She had continued to muse about Nicholas; he was never far away from her thoughts. Milly's cornering her to ask, "Has he called?", or hearing a voice on the radio late at night while she prepared for the next day's classes reminded her of him.

She picked up the skis and poles and headed up the stairs. "I'm off, Mother," she called as she stepped into the kitchen. She was pulling on her gloves when her mother appeared, yawning and tying her robe.

"It's still dark. What are you going to use for headlights?" Jenny asked.

"Don't worry, worrywart. It'll be dawn in another half hour."

"I'm glad Milly's going with you," Jenny said.

"Milly isn't going," Nona said. "When I told her what time I'd pick her up this morning, she changed her mind."

Nona laughed. "Milly said that in her opinion anyone who got up at six o'clock to go skiing had to be a candidate for the crazy farm."

"She might be right," Jenny observed.

"That isn't a very charitable thing to say to me, your darling daughter," Nona stated with magnificent scorn.

Jenny scowled. "It's too darn early in the morning for me to be charitable." She wandered to the counter, flexing her fingers as she walked. "Glad you fixed coffee."

"Fingers stiff?" Nona asked.

Jenny glanced over her shoulder. "Don't worry, worrywart." She sat down at the table.

"Why are you frowning at me, Mother?"

"Milly might be a fashion statement, but you are not. You need a new outfit, Nona."

"I bought this last year. I've only worn it a half a dozen times."

"Gray is so drab-looking. So...utilitarian."

"That's true. But I'm not out to impress anyone."

"I liked that coordinated green outfit you tried on better," Jenny stated.

"So you said at the time," Nona rebutted. "But as I pointed out, the jacket alone cost fifty dollars more than the whole outfit I'm wearing."

"I hate it when you're practical." Jenny laughed. "How long do you plan to be gone?"

"I'm taking the trail through the timber along the Big Sioux River, but I doubt if I'll go all the way to Oak Valley. I should be back by eleven. Have a good day, Mother." She grabbed her skis and poles, and stepped into the brisk morning air.

Because this was her first outing, Nona took the initial mile at a leisurely pace, which enabled her to enjoy the scenery. Dawn was breaking in streaks of red. The trees wore a heavy layer of hoarfrost and reminded her of white-bearded ancients. Birds soared silently overhead. The world was hushed and she loved it.

The second mile, she extended herself and moved briskly. The third mile she slowed again. The outing was cleaning the cobwebs from her mind, she decided. She hadn't thought of Nicholas in an hour.

What had been bothering her since their last meeting was the strangest feeling she got that he'd been trying to make up his mind about her. But *what* about her?

The easiest way to stop thinking about him, she decided, was to start making a list of reasons to dislike him. She laughed. She was flipping out. Whoever heard of talking yourself out of liking someone?

She needed a little change of scenery, a hike through the timber to the river. The weather hadn't been cold enough to freeze the water, so if she went quietly, she might catch birds or animals drinking.

She leaned her poles against a tree, and took off her skis. She picked her way through the trees. When the underbrush behind her rustled, she glanced over her shoulder in time to see a gray rabbit bounding into a clump of dry bromegrass. She continued on, feeling the warmth of the morning sun on her back.

She bent to walk under low-hanging branches but paused before climbing over a fallen tree trunk when she spotted blooming violets growing in the dirt still clinging to the tree roots.

She dropped to her knees for a closer inspection. "They *are* violets," she announced as if she had been in doubt.

She had heard old-timers talk about finding violets in December when they'd gone to the timber to cut firewood or ice from the river, but she'd never seen this quirk of nature herself.

She removed her glove and touched the flowers. So delicate, she thought. The tree roots protected the plant from biting wind and blistering cold, but even so, it seemed a miracle to her that such delicacy could survive.

She tensed. If she didn't know better, she'd think Nicholas was watching her. Utterly impossible. She was probably being watched by an animal. A coon or a fox or a deer. Still, she had to look—and there he was, leaning against a tree, arms folded, smiling at her.

"For heaven's sake." Nona rose and sat on the log. She dusted the snow from her pants, paying no attention to what she was doing because her gaze never left him.

Each time she saw him he looked different. Today he was wearing a brilliant red ski jacket trimmed in black. Black pants. His knit hat was perched rakishly on his black hair. He definitely looked male.

Her mother was right. She should have purchased the green ski outfit, because under his steady gaze she didn't feel "everyday and practical." "What are you doing here?"

"I was cross-country skiing, saw your skis and poles and followed your tracks."

"Those skis could have been anyone's." Nona said. "And don't tell me this is fate or destiny."

"It's true that those skis could have belonged to someone else, but I haven't seen anyone else on the trail. Have you?" he asked.

"No, I haven't."

He shrugged. His eyes sparkled with mischief. "Then it was logical that the skis and poles had to be yours, wasn't it?"

Nona laughed. "Providing you knew before you started out that I was cross-country skiing and where I was headed."

"Yes. Providing I knew."

"Mother—the Alexander answering service?" Nona asked. They were doing it again, bantering while taking quantum leaps in understanding through their gazes. She saw that he was happy to discover she cross-country skied. And he had to see that she was happy he'd found her.

"No less." When he laughed, the sound rippled through the timber.

Nona shivered. She wasn't cold. She was warm, very warm. She smiled and held her breath when he walked toward her.

One moment their gazes were locked and Nona thought he was going to kiss her, the next he had dropped to his knees, taken off his glove and was doing as she'd done, touching the violet.

Nona sighed inwardly. Jon had told her she lacked "fire" sexually, but here she was. She didn't know Nicholas Kendrick, so logic told her she couldn't love him, but he made her so aware of her sexuality. And that was the most stupid thing she'd thought to date. Even if he had searched her out, he wasn't the kind of man who'd skip the social courtesies, pull her into his arms and kiss her.

"The violet is exquisite," he said.

"Ah...yes. It certainly is," Nona agreed. She was lying to him. His eyes were what she thought exquisite.

Nicholas had wanted to kiss her. He had almost kissed her! He couldn't believe himself. He had never been bold.

In high school he had listened with a mixture of disbelief and awe when his peers discussed dating and other sexual adventures. When he had been challenged to elaborate on his prowess, rather than admit he lacked their experience, he'd been silent, allowing them to think whatever they pleased.

The tactic had been quite successful. They'd believed he was more experienced than they, but simply too straight to talk about it. Eventually, he had gained

THE PERFECT WIFE 73

experience. The problem was the experiences hadn't prepared him for Nona.

Now, rather than being stoic, he wished he was daring. He would tell her she was the flower he believed was exquisite. Rosy-cheeked, bright-eyed, her hair softly curling around her blue sock hat. He would tell her he had never been more aware of a woman than he was of her, and never more aware of himself as a man.

"I bribed her," he said, smiling at her and at himself.

"You bribed who?" she asked.

"Your mother," Nicholas said. He stood, intending to move away. Instead, he eased down beside her. "For a twenty-five cent bag of popcorn at the next game I referee, she told me where you'd gone."

Nona smiled. That must have been some conversation he'd had with her mother. "She was cheap."

"That's what she said. I hope you don't mind that I came looking for you."

Nona didn't. But she did. Being alone with him made her more susceptible to the gentle persuasion of his gaze, and she didn't want her resolve to remain only an acquaintance weakened. "Yes, I do mind," she said.

"You do!"

"I said it, didn't I?" Nona asked, wondering what she was going to tell him when he asked why.

"Why?"

Nona chuckled. "I knew you were going to ask me that. Give me a minute to think about it."

She glanced to where two squirrels were chasing each other, circling around and around a tree trunk. That was what her thoughts were doing, chasing each other, never stopping.

"Your minute is up," Nicholas said.

Nona shifted her gaze to him. "I'm not indifferent to you, Nicholas. But every time I see you, I think about Corinne," she said. She stood, paced, then spun to confront him. "I was married to a man who found the qualities he said I lacked in another woman. Call it immaturity on my part, but all I know is I don't like being compared... feeling second-best."

"No one's perfect," Nicholas said. "And any comparing being done is by you." He paused, thinking that wasn't exactly true but he didn't feel like trying to explain. "Would it help if you knew I'm not sure of myself with you, of how I appear to you?"

"It would if I believed it," Nona said. She walked back to the log. Not wanting him to think she was intimidated, she sat exactly where she was sitting. "But I don't," she added, not without a trace of humor.

"Believe it," Nicholas said. "I feel shy and inadequate when I want to be self-assured. And maybe I'd like to be a little macho and mysterious."

"You're pulling it off," she said, sounding breathless. "At least the macho-mysterious part."

Her smile caused Nicholas's heart to knock against his ribs. Self-doubts vanished. "Doing anything special tonight, Nona?"

"Tonight?" Nona asked. "Well, I... Milly—"

"Don't feel obligated to go with me. I know this is late and if you have special plans, I'd understand."

"No, no. I didn't have any special plans."

"Then we've got a date?"

"Yes," she said. "Guess we do."

"I'll pick you up, say six?" Nicholas asked.

"Six will be fine. Mind telling me where we're going? I'd like to know how to dress."

"No need to dress."

"Really?"

Nicholas played it straight in spite of the devilish sparkle in her eyes. "That did sound a little suggestive, didn't it?"

"Not in the least," she said. "But of course I always think on purely platonic levels."

"And of course, being a minister, I do, too," Nicholas said. Or he always had until meeting her.

For a moment, they maintained straight faces, then their laughter whistled like music escaping from a singing teakettle. They leaned closer to each other, their shoulders brushing.

Nicholas gazed into her eyes and wondered if she could be *this* real. Was what he saw—a woman full of vitality, in love with life—what Nona was? Or was he blinded by her beauty and his need to believe she was what he wanted her to be?

He still hadn't answered her question about where they were going, so he said, "You've got a choice. An amateur boxing match or a movie."

Nona noted how his laughter still played in his eyes, ready to dance with the least provocation. "Boxing," she said.

"I was thinking we'd have a late dinner."

"Dinner sounds good," Nona said. She seemed to be the master of understatement lately. Dinner sounded *good*. But she wasn't sure there were dictionary definitions to describe the emotions she'd been feeling since meeting him.

"I wanted to be with you, Nona," he said. "I would have asked you out before this but I was afraid of pushing too hard."

The ardor of his voice heated her, and his gaze caressed her. He slowly lowered his face toward hers, giving her time to turn away, to raise her hands to his chest to stop him, or simply to say no to the beautifully tender request expressed in his eyes.

Her lashes fluttered closed. She was trembling when his lips brushed hers. She didn't question the rightness of kissing him. She simply responded. She was starved for gentle affection, but until now she hadn't known it.

Winter faded. The world warmed. She was not seated on a log next to Nicholas, but lazing at his side on a Caribbean beach.

He didn't embrace her, but tantalized her with his restraint. His mouth moved expertly over hers. She strained toward him. He uttered a sound deep in his chest and touched her cheek with his fingers.

She moaned silently, keeping to herself the effect he was having on her. She savored her feverish excitement. She was aching delightfully. She felt desirable and desired. Above all, because he was gentle, she felt cherished.

THE PERFECT WIFE

She had found here, in the timber on a day in December, the ultimate consummation in a sweet and tender kiss.

She would never again wonder if paradise existed. Paradise was Nicholas's kiss, his touch. She raised her ungloved hand to his face, memorized the slightly rough texture of his skin, the contour of his cheek, the outline of his ear.

The joy she felt brought tears to her eyes and moistened her lashes. She had been without spirit and fire until this moment.

His shudder brought reality crashing back. Nona lowered her hand.

"Should I apologize?" he asked.

His lips were only a delicious breath away. "No. Don't apologize," Nona whispered.

She opened her eyes, and the surprise and alarm in his expression made her wonder if she shouldn't be the one to apologize. She was a surrogate for Corinne, and he'd just realized it.

"I know why you kissed me," she said. "Don't worry about it."

"Worry about it?" he asked. "I apologized because I thought I might have been too aggressive."

Nona averted her gaze. He had a very strange idea of aggressiveness. "Like I said, don't worry about it." She paused, then stammered, "I know—well—I suppose it's been a long..." She faltered to a stop, met his gaze. "You know."

"A long time since I kissed a woman," he supplied quietly.

"Yes," she said. "So I understand why you kissed me. I'm a surrogate...kind of...and I'm so darned embarrassed. I'm saying this so badly."

He touched her cheek with his fingertips again. "Corinne is often on my mind. I can't deny that, but it was you, your lips that gave me a taste of heaven, Nona. Your lips. No surrogate, kind of or otherwise. Your lips."

Nona couldn't think clearly when he was touching her. She couldn't think clearly even after he'd lowered his hand. "I don't know what you want from me," she said. "What is it?"

"It isn't sex, if that's what you're thinking," he said.

The words hung between them for a weighted moment. "Now that you've brought the subject up. I'm against it," Nona said.

"Against lovemaking?"

His gaze was tickling her. It was delightful. "You know exactly what I meant," she said.

"I know what you meant. And rest assured, as far as trysting goes, this is as far as I go," he said. "Kissing you deep in the timber where only the animals and birds can witness it."

With a few sweetly wicked words, he had eased the tension she'd been feeling. "Or you could say kissing me deeply deep in the timber."

He arched a brow. "I can do better."

"I don't know if I could handle better."

They laughed. Then he said seriously, "I didn't answer when you asked what I wanted from you. Do we have to know at this particular moment where we're headed?"

"I'd feel better in my own mind if I had some idea," Nona said honestly. Her mother's words rang in her head... yearned to talk to talk to your father... "Companionship," she suggested.

"Companionship certainly. Friendship," he added. He tilted his head and arched a brow. "And an occasional kiss?"

"You aren't worried about appearances," Nona stated.

"The ninety-nine percent that you talked about, those are the people whose opinions are important, if others' opinions are important, at all. I believe in the basic good of people," he said. "They won't fault us for finding companionship wherever we can."

Wherever we can? Nona felt his words had depersonalized her, though she knew he hadn't intended it. Hadn't intended to hurt her feelings. He was only being honest.

She'd yearned for male companionship after her divorce, just as her mother had yearned for male companionship after her father had died. So Nicholas's need was understandable. As long as that was all he was looking for in a woman, she could handle that... couldn't she?

"Okay. We're on for companionship," she said cheerfully. She stuck out her hand. "Put it there, buddy."

Chapter Six

Grinning, Nicholas took her hand. "Ready to ski again?" he asked as he stood, then pulled her to her feet.

"You bet. Are you interested in racing?"

Nicholas could buy that. He needed to expend a lot of energy. All his calm talk about an occasional kiss—what a bunch of phoney baloney, as his mother liked to say. He was still sensitized, still battling the effects of the kiss they had shared.

"I love to race. Are you challenging me?" he asked.

"Yes, I am," Nona said. She started walking back through the timber.

He moved at her side, feeling marvelous. Life should always be so good. "I accept," he said.

She looked at him. "I must say your grin borders on

the sanguine, Nicholas. Just how good a skier are you—ardently confident or simply optimistic?"

"I'm pretty good. How good are you?"

"Terrific!"

Nicholas laughed. "Indeed you are. I'll bet you're even a good skier."

She smiled. "Flattery will get you nowhere."

After putting on their skis, they designated a fence a mile away as the finish and took off. With about three hundred more feet to go, he glanced over his shoulder. She was no more than a hundred feet behind him and moving easily. She glanced up, smiled confidently. He returned the smile as confidently.

She had endurance. He hoped his lasted.

It did, barely. He was leaning on his poles, catching his breath when she slid up. "You're terrific all right," he said.

"You beat me, so what does that make you?"

He bent and kissed her flushed cheek. "The winner," he said.

Hours later, Nicholas watched her ski home. They had spent the first hour dueling. He had bestowed three winner's kisses on her cheek—and had been the recipient of one.

His physical response to her was extraordinary and that was putting it mildly. Each time he had kissed her, touched her, his body was pierced by hot slivers of desire. He'd felt nothing like it before.

He had been thinking he had to leave when they had given up dueling. They had spent the last hour skiing side-by-side. Her conversation had sparkled, her blue eyes often expressing her emotions before she expressed them verbally.

And there had been long silences between them. But the silences hadn't been filled with tension. They'd communicated through smiles and nods. He'd nodded toward a different path closer to the river, asking if they should take it, and she'd nodded back in agreement. They'd shared spontaneous laughter when they'd come upon two blue jays squabbling over feeding territory. The birds took short, jerky flights at each other, ignoring their human audience.

It was during one of those long silences that he understood why the silences were comfortable. Nona trusted him.

He didn't want to betray her trust. He prayed for guidance.

Jenny was in the kitchen when Nona stepped inside. "Soup's ready."

Nona glanced at the clock. Noon! "I didn't realize it was that late! I'm not really hungry, Mother," she said apologetically. "I'd better shower or I'm going to be late for basketball practice."

"Nicholas found you." Jenny turned off the burner under the soup.

"Yes," Nona said. "He found me." She headed for the stairs.

Jenny followed her. "What happened?"

Nona looked over her shoulder. "You're nosy."

"I know I'm nosy. Why did he want to see you, other than because you happen to be vivacious, charming and witty?"

"He wanted to ask me to watch boxing with him. Tonight. Six o'clock," Nona said. "Mother, will you do me a favor? Call Milly and tell her I can't go out with her tonight."

"She'll ask why."

"I trust Milly. Tell her."

"It's going to cost you a fifty-cent bag of popcorn at the next basketball game."

"You settled on a twenty-five cent bag from Nicholas."

"It would have cost you less if you'd been more forthcoming on what you were doing this morning," Jenny quipped, then turned serious. "You do know that this is how it starts, don't you?"

"What is *it*?"

"Love. Love starts with eyes bright with remembered, shared laughter. Time flying. A secretive attitude. Lord, I wish I were twenty again!"

"My mother, the romantic."

"My daughter, the pragmatist," Jenny countered. "But there's hope for you, Nona. Pragmatists are pragmatists only until they fall in love."

Nona laughed as she scurried up the stairs. Of course her mother could see how much she already cared about Nicholas. Nona wasn't concerned about that. What did concern her was wondering if she had the ability to keep Nicholas from knowing how much she cared.

She understood why he wanted to be with her, and accepted it. He was lonely, in need of companionship. And companionship wasn't too much of one human being to ask of another. But she couldn't complicate the situation for him by being anymore to him than what he wanted—a friend.

But oh joy! She had spent an *entire* morning with Nicholas. She was going on a date with Nicholas. He'd wanted her to be with him.

Had she ever felt so wonderful, so filled with energy?

"Nona, Nicholas is here," Jenny called up the stairs.

"Be down in a minute," Nona called back. Her fingers shook as she tried to clasp her gold link necklace. Usually, she dressed quickly and efficiently, and managed to look fine, even attractive.

However, getting dressed tonight had been torment. The only requirement when she started was her determination to wear a dress. Nicholas had never seen her in a dress.

It went downhill from there. Every dress she had tried on, everything she had done with her hair and makeup, she had wondered what Nicholas would think.

The necklace in place, she moved to the full-length mirror and evaluated herself critically. She had settled on wearing a simple blue jersey with a V neckline, slightly puffed shoulders, long sleeves and full skirt.

The darn thing! It showed no curves on her chest where she assured herself she had some and it ballooned over her hips, which she knew carried only a thin layer of fat.

It was all wrong!

"Nona! Did you drown in the bathtub?"

"I'm coming, Mother!" She didn't have time to change.

"Good," Jenny yelled. "I've been showing Nicholas your baby pictures and I was about to embarrass you by showing him the one of you on the bearskin rug!"

"You don't have a picture of me on a bearskin rug," she called. "That's a picture of Lillian."

She heard her mother explain that Lillian was a younger daughter. Then she heard Nicholas's muffled laughter and her heart pounded. Her hands grew cold, her lips dry. It was a classic case of panic. She moistened her lips with her tongue and grabbed her coat from the bed.

She didn't want to step from the sanctuary of her bedroom out into the hall. Yes, she did! She was aching to see Nicholas. But what was she going to say to him? Could they pick up from where they had left off this morning, easily exchanging bits of information, visiting... brushing friendly kisses on each other's cheeks...

Nicholas held Nona's elbow as they walked down the sidewalk. The temperatures had risen to the mid-thirties during the day and the snow had melted. Now the water had frozen and the footing was dangerous.

He opened his car's passenger door. "I didn't want to say this in front of your mother, but I'm glad you dressed," he said, his voice low. "You... and the dress... are beautiful."

"Thank you," Nona said. She slid inside and watched him walk around. She thought he looked pretty good himself. Under his winter coat he was wearing a dark brown leisure suit.

"Can you guess," he said once he was seated, "how nervous this makes me?"

He drove toward the highway. In the dim lighting provided by the dash, his expression appeared apprehensive.

Had he reconsidered his position? "Are you having second thoughts?" she asked.

"About what?"

"About asking me along," Nona said. "It's not too late to back out."

"Why would I want to do that?"

"You just said this was making you nervous."

"I should have said *you* make me nervous."

It was beyond belief she could make him nervous, but he was obviously nervous about something. "Well, you make me a bit nervous, too," she admitted. "I'm not quite sure whether or not I used mascara on both eyes."

His laugh was so soft Nona could barely hear it. "You did both eyes, Nona," he said. "And your light blue eye shadow is perfect."

Nona's breathing quickened. As she had come down the stairs, she had seen him take inventory of her. And she had seen approval in his eyes. But his noting details like the eye shadow she'd applied so lightly it was barely visible unnerved her.

In truth, quite a lot about him unnerved her, but he didn't seem to notice she hadn't responded. He continued to speak.

"It's been a long time since I dated," he was saying. "I wasn't very good at it. I think that's why I'm nervous. How about you?"

Thank goodness he could be calm and candid about it. He was saving her from an awkward moment. "It's been a long time since I had a date."

He glanced at her. She felt herself blush. "I can't believe I admitted that," she said, laughing.

"You must have been asked," he stated. "So why has it been a long time?"

Nona shifted. "Lots of reasons," she said. "A lack of men I shared common interests with. Mostly because too many men have a singular objective in mind."

"Men not interested in bonding emotionally but physically?" he asked.

"Nicely put," Nona said. "I've found it's easier to say no when I'm asked for a date, rather than to say no in the middle. Especially if I really didn't want to go in the first place but might have allowed myself to be talked into it."

He laughed. "But you said yes to me because you trust me."

He'd used that low tone of voice Nona'd come to think of as provocative. She met his gaze. "Shouldn't I?" she asked.

"I'll need watching," he said chuckling.

A car passed them, honking, and going too fast for the icy road conditions, Nona thought.

"You do represent temptation—I should recognize that car."

"Try anything and I'll twist your arm—oh, my god!" She gasped.

Ahead of them, the car was fishtailing.

Nicholas threw his right arm protectively across Nona's chest—Nona thought the action was endearing—and stopped his car.

They groaned in unison when the other car spun in a half circle, its headlights dancing eerily on the trees growing in a pasture. It hit the hard-packed snow ridge left by a snow plow, rolled to its side, skidded, bounced back on its wheels and came to rest nose-to-nose with Nicholas's car.

"Are you all right?" Nicholas asked.

"Sure," she murmured while Nicholas was saying, "I think it's the Timmonses."

"Oh, no," Nona whispered. The roof on the driver's side was caved in.

Nicholas got out and walked over. Nona was on his heels. He tried the driver's door. It wouldn't open. He pounded on the window. "Ralph! It's me. Nicholas."

The man turned his head slowly. In the dull light, his eyes showed no recognition. "He's alive," Nicholas said, relief sounding in his voice.

"I'll take your car and go for help. A family called the Buttles live on the next farm," Nona said.

"I'm not having you risk your neck. I'll go just as soon as I check on Agnes." He was reaching for the passenger door when it opened. "Agnes. Thank God," he said. "Don't move!" he warned her when it appeared she was trying to struggle from her seat.

"Reverend Kendrick, I think Ralph is hurt bad," Agnes mumbled. She lifted up her hand. Nicholas dropped to his knees, took her hand in his and gently restrained her with the other.

"Listen to me. Nona Alexander is with me. She'll stay with you while I go to call the ambulance."

"No! No! Don't leave us," Agnes cried. She clutched his hand.

Nicholas looked up at Nona.

"I'll go. You're needed here," Nona said.

"Nona—"

Behind his calmness, Nona saw fear. Corinne had died in a car accident. "Don't worry. I drive on ice every winter," she said.

He nodded, whispered, "Okay. But be careful."

Nona flew to the car. It seemed like hours before she turned into the driveway of the farm half a mile away, an infinity before Hortense, hard of hearing, answered the knock on the door. Another infinity while she explained at the top of her voice that she needed to use the telephone and why. And still another lifetime before she'd called the emergency number and was told help was on its way.

Nona thanked Hortense, but before she could escape from the kitchen, Luke Buttles woke from napping before the television in the front room and walked into the kitchen asking what all the noise was about.

All Nona could think about was that Nicholas needed her help and she needed to be with him. She made the explanation in two sentences and said goodbye. The moment she'd closed the door behind her, she heard the siren of the ambulance coming out of

Beaver Crossing, then the fire truck. They were no more than six miles from town. "Hurry. Hurry," she whispered.

She shivered and pulled the fur collar of her coat up around her ears. She carefully picked her way back to Nicholas's car, which for the first time she noticed was a bit unusual for a preacher, at least in color. It was white. Not many ministers she knew drove white cars.

Once inside, she took a deep breath. The car smelled faintly of Nicholas's spicy after-shave. Her trembling eased. Had she been shivering against the cold, or from panic? Had it been the warmth of the car that stopped the shivering, or was it the scent of cologne, a reminder of Nicholas and his steady bearing in the face of a crisis... that had to remind him of another crisis...

Nona had leafed through two magazines in the emergency-ward reception area while waiting for Nicholas. She walked to the coffee brewer and drew a cup. With her first sip, she knew that had been a mistake.

She turned toward the woman who'd been sharing the waiting room with her. She hadn't given Nona a chance to strike up a conversation, but when she glanced up from the magazine she was reading, Nona took the opening.

"This coffee must have been brewed yesterday," she said with a laugh.

The dark-haired woman, mid-fifties, Nona guessed, returned to her reading. "It's free, isn't it?" She said tersely.

Nona didn't think the lady would ever win a Ms. Congeniality award. She dumped the coffee, then walked over to look out the window, discreetly studying the woman as she went. She felt she should recognize her.

At the window, she turned. "I don't mean to interrupt your reading, but you look familiar. I feel as if I should know you."

The woman looked up but didn't meet Nona's gaze. "You should. I'm Adeline Drew. I met you two years ago. You and your mother attended the retirement party for Reverend Lockhart." She went back to reading.

Nona nodded. Reverend Lockhart had been the minister at Oak Valley. Before Nicholas, there had been another elderly man.

Nicholas stepped into the room, looking relieved. He crossed to Nona, slipped his arm around her waist and kissed her on the cheek.

"The Timmonses are going to be fine," he said and stepped away. "Agnes has a couple of broken ribs and a broken arm, Ralph a concussion and a broken leg. Barring complications, they'll be fine."

"I don't know how they lived through it," Nona murmured. "Has their daughter arrived?"

"Tessa and her husband are with the Timmonses right now," he said. He paused as if sensing someone else was in the room, then turned. "Well, Adeline." Adeline looked up. "Adeline," Nicholas said, "this is Nona Alexander. Nona. Adeline Drew."

"Met," Adeline said.

Nona grimaced. "Adeline and I met at Reverend Lockhart's retirement party."

"Really?" Nicholas asked. He glanced back to Adeline, who was turning a page of the magazine. "Well... Adeline, what are you doing here?"

Adeline closed the magazine, using a finger to mark her place. "Waiting to see whether or not they'll keep Tom overnight, Reverend Kendrick." She spoke through pinched lips. "My son's ulcer is acting up again. What happened to the Timmonses?"

Nicholas quickly explained. Adeline's upper lip twitched. "Ralph Timmons has never been known to be a good driver. Especially when he's been drinking."

"He wasn't drinking, Adeline," Nicholas said calmly. He smiled.

But Nona felt he was barely controlling his temper, which was why she wasn't saying anything. She felt like tweaking Adeline's nose so the woman would really have something to be bent out of shape over.

"What room is Tom in?" Nicholas asked. "Maybe I could drop—"

"He's sleeping," Adeline said. She opened her magazine again, effectively ending the conversation.

"See you in church tomorrow, Adeline," Nicholas said cheerfully.

"Hum," Adeline said.

Nona was first into the hall.

"It's only ten o'clock," Nicholas said as he joined her. "We can still make a couple of matches. You game?"

Nona had to force cheerfulness into her voice. Adeline couldn't be trusted. "Let's go."

As they walked out, they put on their coats and gloves.

"Adeline Drew does go to your church," she said.

Nicholas looked up. "Every Sunday."

"She saw you kiss me."

"So?"

Nona couldn't shake the foreboding feeling. "I don't trust her, Nicholas."

"The events of this evening have been upsetting," he assured her.

Nona wanted to believe that was what was behind the portent of doom she sensed. She really did. But she couldn't forget the look on Adeline's face when Nicholas had kissed her. She hadn't been able to tell what Adeline had been thinking, but Nona knew whatever it was, she didn't like it.

Yet when Nicholas slipped his arm over her shoulder and they stepped into the cold night together, her apprehension disappeared.

Chapter Seven

The entertainment for Nicholas was not in the ring, but Nona. She had slipped into her own little world, intent on the match, participating in a way that both surprised and enchanted him.

They had arrived in the middle of a heavyweight bout. Nona had immediately championed a dark-haired young man because he was wearing blue trunks. Through the rounds, she feinted left and parried right, trying to spur her boxer to victory. She grunted when he got hit with a hard jab to the midsection, and cheered when he jabbed back.

As he watched her, the sensations he'd experienced that morning when he'd kissed her, returned—but with more intensity, which he would never have believed possible.

"Do you think the fight is fair?" he asked.

THE PERFECT WIFE

"Fair?" she asked without taking her eyes off the action. "Of course it's fair."

"How can you say it's fair?" Nicholas asked. "The poor guy in the red trunks is fighting the guy in the blue—and you."

She gave him a playful look of rebuke. He started laughing until he was in tears. He wiped them away, then glanced at Nona. How could she tell he'd found it? The spontaneity he had once had, and lost when he'd learned to control his emotions.

She smiled, almost knowingly, then looked back at the ring, gasped and covered her eyes.

"Now what are you doing?" he asked.

"I like boxing. But I can't stand to see a nosebleed."

"Well, your man definitely has a nosebleed," Nicholas appraised.

"What's happening?" she yelled over the screams of the crowd.

"More blood. Only it's the other guy's," Nicholas said before he realized her fingers were trembling. He lowered her hands, turned her face to him. "I'm sorry, Nona. I thought you were teasing."

Nona tried to smile. In defense of herself, she explained, "A nosebleed has bothered me ever since my sister Natalie broke her nose."

The crowd roared. The young man in the red trunks was down, the referee bending over him, arm swinging in the count. The referee gestured the ring men in to assist the groggy fighter. Moments later, he stood center ring with the blue-trunked fighter's hand raised while the announcer bellowed, "Ladies and gentlemen. If I could have your attention. The winner of the fight: Battlin' Billy. Next fight: ten minutes."

Nona smiled. "Guess a little nosebleed didn't stop him," she said.

"Guess not. What about Natalie?" Nicholas asked.

"She was five. The youngest. We were in the backyard playing. Mother was working. I was in charge of the kids. I turned around and there Natalie was, perched about ten feet off the ground in a cottonwood tree. And then, there she was falling," Nona said. "The next thing I knew blood was spurting from her nose."

"You must have been scared," Nicholas observed.

Nona half chuckled. "Scared? Terrified. I was responsible for the kids. I knew I'd *have* to tell Mother because if I didn't one of the kids would squeal on me. I cried every step of the way to Doc Summer's office and once I'd handed Natalie over, I promptly passed out."

Nicholas smiled sympathetically. "You cried because Natalie was hurt and you felt responsible. I'm glad the story had a happy ending. You got Natalie to the doctor before you passed out."

"It turned out okay for her, but I hit a chair going down," Nona said, feigning petulance. "Blackened my eye. Natalie hurt for a week. I was bruised for a month."

Nicholas rested his arm on her shoulder. "Poor baby," he crooned in her ear.

"You don't sound very sympathetic to me," Nona said. His casual embrace made every nerve ending in her body act like radar all honed in on him.

"What happens when one of the girls gets a nosebleed, skins a shin during practice or a game?"

"A skinned shin is no problem. Luckily, on the two occasions when someone has had a nosebleed, Mel and Milly have been there. I let them handle it while I pretend to be busy with other things."

"Nona, there simply aren't any circumstances you can't handle," he stated. "I witnessed that earlier tonight. You were calm—"

"Calm? Like when I screamed?" she asked.

"You don't think I was screaming?" Nicholas asked. "The only reason you didn't hear me was because I was so scared I couldn't get it out."

He kissed her cheek and felt her warmth. What she did to him... "I needed your strength tonight," he whispered, then teased, "Good thing neither of the Timmonses had a nosebleed, huh?"

"You'd have had me on your hands, too, for sure," she said. "I get woozy every time. Let's change the subject or I'll lose my appetite for dinner."

He pulled her close. "It's all right. Even if you're a wimp when it comes to a little you-know-what, I like you anyway."

Oh, land, Nona thought. She was reading too much into the fondling sound of his voice, the soft look in his eyes, his strong fingers kneading her shoulder.

"What can I say after a compliment like that but thanks," she said.

"Let's get out of here," Nicholas suggested.

"There's one fight left on the card."

"I want to talk with you without having to yell," he yelled over the crowd, which was greeting the next boxers.

They were seated at a table next to a window in a restaurant in downtown Sioux City. The restaurant was located on the top floor of one of the tallest buildings in the city, giving them a view of the city, resplendent with Christmas lights. A bank building nearby was outlined in twinkling green, the clock tower in red. The trees in the mall sparkled with white lights.

"Beautiful sight," Nicholas said.

"I was just thinking myself how festive it looks," Nona said.

Nicholas smiled. No matter what they were doing, what they were saying, there was an undercurrent of understanding flowing between them.

"With all that's gone on tonight," he observed, "I've worked up a hefty appetite," he said. When her gaze met his, he asked, "How's your appetite?"

"I can tell by that fiendish twinkle in your eyes exactly what you're thinking, Nicholas. But don't you dare bring up the subject of you-know-what before I order or I'll think you lack compassion."

"Maybe I'm not as compassionate as you think," he said, trying to sound lighthearted.

"You demonstrated compassion tonight with the Timmonses," Nona said sincerely.

Nicholas's thoughts splintered. He'd told himself he was not going to think about Corinne tonight, but being with Nona warmed his soul in a wonderful way and he couldn't help but question why his heart had hardened toward Corinne. Even if she hadn't been loving, shouldn't he have been capable of finding good in her and appreciating that?

"Is something troubling you, Nicholas?" Nona asked.

"I could say nothing is bothering me. But since Corinne died, there have been moments when I've wondered if I'm worthy of my vocation," he admitted.

"For what it's worth," she offered, "you admit your doubts. Most of us can't. You question your worthiness. Most of us are too complacent to care."

"You care, Nona," Nicholas said. He loved the musical sound of her name. Loved the way she blushed softly when given a compliment. "Now, what are you going to have to eat?"

"I think..." She pursed her lips, then looked up. "Let's perform a little experiment. You try to pick out something you think I'd like to eat and I'll tell you whether or not I like it."

"You'll never succeed at being devious. You scanned the menu and thought, 'My goodness. Everything is so expensive for the budget of a minister.'"

"You're right," she admitted.

Nicholas chuckled. "I appreciate your concern, but I have enough money in my pocket to buy a meal for my buddy."

Nona smiled, but her thoughts were anything but light. She was very aware of the sensual undertones in his voice, of the way his gaze touched her—and very aware that he was torn. There were things he wanted to tell her, but couldn't share. Too intimate? she wondered.

"I'll have the lobster," she said.

Nicholas mocked a groan. "Did I say order the most expensive item?"

"Don't make blustering boasts if you don't intend to follow through." She gave him an impish grin. "I'll stick with the lobster."

Nicholas laughed. When the waitress came, he ordered two lobsters and white wine. After the wine came, he directed Nona's attention out the window to a plane with its landing lights on, flying low over the city.

"Ever look at a train or plane and wonder where the people have been or are going?" he asked. He sipped the wine.

"Always," Nona said.

She was running a fingertip around the rim of her glass, down the stem...and he felt her fingertip roaming over his face.

He cleared his throat. "Uh...have you traveled much?"

"Not as much as I would have liked. First there was college and I couldn't afford to travel. Then—" she shifted her gaze from him to stare out the window "—after I was married, Jon and I differed about the kinds of vacations we wanted to take." She shrugged. "We took separate vacations."

"Let me guess. You found some backwoods retreat and spent your time fishing. Reading. Swimming. Jogging. And visiting with the local people," he said.

"Exactly. How did you know?"

"Because I like to spend my vacations at a backwoods retreat," he said.

The sensual intensity of his voice made Nona feel as if she were working out on an emotional treadmill. Just as she felt in control of the situation, he would "turn the speed up" on her. Did everything he said have to sound evocative? Or was it her imagination?

"Are there places you'd like to see someday?" she asked, sounding casual.

"Canada. How about you?"

"Alaska."

"Why are you waiting for someday, Nona? You could travel during the summer."

"I've discovered I don't like to travel alone." Nona toyed with her napkin, looked across the table at him from under lowered lashes. She added with a straight face, "I'm not quite ready to go on a bus tour with a lot of other old maids, but I suppose that day will come."

Nona had intended for Nicholas to laugh. When he didn't, she said, "That was a joke. You were supposed to laugh."

"I know it was a joke," Nicholas said. "But it didn't strike me as funny, hearing you insinuate you don't plan to remarry."

Without warning, he reached across the table and touched Nona's cheek. Her nerve radar activated, and she was besieged with warnings. She had hoped to fall in love and marry someday. And it didn't seem fair that Nicholas was the one who could stir those thoughts to a frenzy with a simple touch. Not fair that even after he lowered his hand to the table, her cheek still tingled with desire for his caress.

"I wasn't insinuating that I wouldn't get married," she said carefully. "But I don't think a person *plans* to remarry. To plan to remarry puts marriage in the same category as planning to purchase a new sofa after the old sofa has worn out."

"Agreed," Nicholas said. "I was only pointing out that you should be open to the possibility of falling in love again."

"How open are *you* to the possibility of falling in love again?" Nona asked, then realized how uncaring she'd sounded. She added quickly. "I'm sorry, Nicholas. That wasn't a kind question to ask under the circumstances."

"I think the question was fair enough. But I don't honestly know," he said. "I guess the only thing I could say would be time will tell."

"That's where I am," Nona said. "Time will tell."

"Say if this is none of my business," Nicholas said slowly, "but were you ever happy in your marriage?"

"I thought I was happy," Nona admitted without hesitation. "It was only after I was divorced that I realized I hadn't been happy but complacent. Now, even if I thought I was in love I'd give my feelings a real study before I made that kind of commitment again."

Nicholas covered her hand with his, then entwined his fingers with hers. Nona had thought they were going to have an unemotional discussion. But he'd done it to her again. She was completely unhinged.

"So you have no lingering regrets?" he asked gently.

Nona didn't want to answer. She wanted to relish the feeling of his strong fingers on hers.

"Only one. My relationship with the Alexanders," she said softly. "After the divorce, well, they were obviously uncomfortable whenever I was around. I don't know. There didn't seem to be anything to say."

"Is there something you wished you'd said to the Alexanders?"

"Are you sermonizing?"

"Did it sound like sermonizing?"

"It did, but you do it splendidly. Yes. There are things I'd like to say to Emily and Jon, Sr. First and foremost that my feelings for them haven't changed," she said. "I still love them. So I'm going to consider calling them. Thank you for pointing out that inaction solves nothing."

Suddenly Nona realized all the talking they had been doing seemed to be about her. "What was Corinne like, personality-wise?" she asked gently.

Nicholas withdrew his hand, shifted on the chair, then turned his gaze from her to stare out the window. "I want to be honest with you about her," he said. He looked back at Nona. "But there's nothing I could say that would be objective."

He hadn't been curt, but Nona got the message. There were some things about Corinne that he was not going to share with her. Those personal, intimate details that made a good marriage. She understood, but in ways she didn't. It hurt knowing there were feelings he couldn't share with her.

"I understand," she was saying when the waitress came with their salads. As they ate, the conversation turned superficial, light again. Eventually they were discussing what they did to relax.

When he mentioned he did some sketching, she said, "I suppose you're as good at drawing as you are at cross-country skiing."

He chuckled. "Yes, Nona, I am."

"I knew it. Isn't there anything you aren't good at doing? Figuratively speaking, one mountain you can't climb?"

"The worst kind of mountain," he said slowly, "is the one I've built in my own mind. When I question my worthiness, my humanness, my compassion. That's a mountain. And there have been times when I doubt my ability to climb it."

This was the second time Nicholas had expressed a lack of faith in himself. But this time she was stunned into silence by the grief in his face. She'd grieved when her father died, and had watched her mother's grieving, but she had never witnessed the hopeless kind of grief Nicholas was displaying.

Feeling helpless, she placed her hand on his and gently stroked it.

Nona and Nicholas were laughing when they had parted at her door at two A.M. And she'd accepted his invitation to lunch that same day without the slightest hesitation. Now, as she raised her hand to knock on his front door, she wondered what had possessed her.

He hadn't kissed her last night, but she'd seen he had wanted to kiss her. She was ambivalent because after their dinner conversation she had started wondering all over again who Nicholas saw when he looked at her, who he thought he was talking to, who he wanted in his arms. So she hadn't encouraged him. And he hadn't taken the initiative.

The door was thrown open and Ivy appeared, a smile on her face. "Nona, come in. I'm so happy Nicholas invited you to lunch."

Nona stepped inside and shut the door behind her. "I hope such short notice wasn't an inconvenience," she said, taking off her coat.

"Heaven's, no," Ivy said. She put Nona's coat in the hall closet.

Nona glanced around. Typical parsonage. Pleasant, but neat to the point of being sterile. "Nicholas and Kelly are still at church," Ivy said. "He had a short choir practice with the youth group. They're going caroling."

"By the way, Tessa called early this morning to say her parents had a good night."

"That's wonderful. I still shake when I think about the accident," Nona said. She followed Ivy into the kitchen.

"Have a chair. I'm working on the salad." Ivy walked over to the counter. "I didn't know until Adeline Drew told me that you'd gone with Nicholas to the hospital."

Nona had been wondering if she'd dressed inappropriately for lunch. After church, she'd changed into slacks. Ivy was wearing a dark blue dress with a lace collar, and she had on a frilly peach-colored apron.

But thoughts of clothes suddenly seemed frivolous as the picture of Adeline's lips pursed in a display of displeasure flashed through Nona's mind.

"How is Adeline's son?" Nona asked.

"Okay, I guess. At least he was in church today," Ivy said. She looked up, smiling. "Nicholas wouldn't like it if he heard me saying this, but living with Adeline would give anyone an ulcer."

Nona agreed. But apparently Adeline hadn't said anything more to Ivy than that she'd seen her with Nicholas. "Please, Ivy," Nona said. "Let me help you with lunch."

"Everything is ready but the salad. The casserole will be done in fifteen minutes." She turned to Nona. "But you could set the table."

"Fine," Nona said.

She followed Ivy into the dining room where a harvest table held center stage. Ivy pointed out the china—displayed in an antique cabinet—and the silver, then returned to the kitchen.

"It was Nicholas's idea," Ivy called out.

Nona was admiring the china, white with a delicate leaf pattern in earth colors along the edges. "What was Nicholas's idea?" she asked.

"The caroling. He's also planning to have the group here for cocoa and sandwiches after. He sometimes forgets..."

Nona placed the last of the plates on the table. She stepped to the door. "I'm sorry, Ivy, I didn't catch the last of what you were saying."

"You didn't miss it," Ivy admitted. She broke the lettuce apart with quick, precise movements. "What I was going to say sounded critical of Nicholas and I don't want to be. But he sometimes forgets it's me, not Corinne trying to get everything done."

"I imagine Nicholas knows you're trying," Nona offered sympathetically.

Ivy laughed. For the first time Nona saw some of the sparkle of mischief in her eyes, which so readily surfaced in Nicholas's. "I do try. But I have only so much *try* in me and when Nicholas said, 'Oh, by the way, Ivy. On the twenty-second of December, we'll be having thirty or thirty-five young people for lunch after caroling, but don't worry, I'll take care of it,' I came close to hitting him."

"And I haven't hit him since he got big enough to hit me back."

Their laughter had dwindled to giggling when Nicholas walked into the kitchen through the back door. "I missed something," he said.

Nona was caught in an emotional whiplash. His grin begged continued laughter, but his dress for the pulpit—black suit, vest and shirt, white collar—while striking, caused her to reflect with sobriety that this was Nicholas Kendrick: a man of God.

He was a special kind of man who needed a special kind of woman to share his life with. As Ivy had expressed her frustration, Nona had been sharply reminded of her own shortcomings as a wife.

She put a mental stranglehold on the tug at her heart. Though she had known it last night as he and

Agnes prayed, this time she *felt* the significance. Friendship was all there could be between Nicholas Kendrick and herself.

And she knew in her heart even that was risky.

"You missed nothing," she said.

Chapter Eight

After dinner, Nona and Nicholas helped Kelly build a snowman, and ended up in a snowball fight, which Nona won after Kelly sided with her. Kelly was in high spirits as she left to go sledding on a nearby hill with children from a neighboring farm.

As Nona and Nicholas stepped into the house, boots in hand, Ivy called from the den down the hall, "I fixed some coffee. If you don't mind, I'll leave you people to get it. I'm doing cards."

"Thank you, Ivy. We will," Nicholas said. He hung his coat, then reached for Nona's.

"I should be going," Nona said thoughtfully. "I have several hours of preparation ahead for tomorrow's classes."

"Stay a few minutes longer," Nicholas said. "We haven't had a chance to talk."

Nona knew what he meant. They had been talking for hours, but always with someone around. Still, sometime during lunch Nona had affirmed in her mind that no matter how much he needed her friendship, the best thing to do would be to limit the time they spent together.

However, under his steady gaze, she wavered.

"I thought you were going to Sioux City to see the Timmonses," she suggested.

"I am. But I'd planned to go later." He took her coat and hung it in the closet. "Go on into the front room. I'll get the coffee and be with you in a minute. Want a cookie?"

"No, thank you," Nona said.

Nicholas disappeared down the hall. Nona wandered into the front room and settled on the sofa. She gazed around the room at the walls, the television set, the built-in bookshelves, not realizing until her search was done that she'd been looking for a picture of Corinne. There was none.

Nicholas came back. He handed her a steaming cup of coffee, then settled across the room on an overstuffed chair. Here we are, Nona thought. Just the two of us. And I don't know what to say.

"I meant to ask you last night how the team has done the last two weeks," Nicholas said.

Nona blew on her coffee to cool it. Thank goodness, he wanted to visit about ordinary things. "They're four and four now."

"Not bad for a team with so little experience," Nicholas said. "You're a good coach and the girls want to win for you as well as for themselves. I think they'll end with a winning season."

"Mel has a lot to do with the improvement the girls are showing," Nona said. "But we're having a passing problem with Tracy Freemont."

"I suppose you've demonstrated what you want her to do?" Nicholas asked, smiling.

Nona laughed. "You would not believe how I've demonstrated, but she acts as if she hasn't the vaguest idea what to do."

"Maybe you intimidate her," Nicholas suggested.

Nona scoffed. "I don't intimidate anyone."

"On occasion, you intimidate me."

Nona narrowed her eyes and studied him stretched out casually in the chair. He had changed before lunch into snug-fitting jeans and a blue crewneck sweater. His gaze was anything but timid.

She tried to sound unaffected. "Sir, you display anything but diffidence."

"That, Nona, is your opinion," Nicholas said.

With her he hesitated, not as much as he had yesterday or when they'd first met. But he did hesitate. And he wished he could get over this feeling that he was going to do or say something that would diminish her respect for him. And last night! Last night he almost confessed what was driving him. He had reason to hesitate, all right.

"If I recall correctly," he said, "when Tracy's in control of the ball, she's tentative." He set his cup aside, leaned an elbow on the arm of the chair.

"That's her problem in a nutshell," Nona said. "I'd hoped game experience would give her confidence in herself, but I'm beginning to think she simply doesn't have a competitive nature. Any ideas?"

"Bring in one of the boys for practice," Nicholas offered thoughtfully before baiting her. "Nothing brings out the tigress in the weaker sex quicker than being in competition with—or for—the stronger sex."

"Really?" Nona asked, pursing her lips. She set her cup on the coffee table.

Nicholas saw by the flash in Nona's eyes that she'd risen to the bait. Or was close to it. "It's a fact," Nicholas said.

"I believe it has been scientifically proven that the female of any species is anatomically superior to the male," she retorted.

Looking at her, there was no way Nicholas would argue the point. Her blouse dipped into a vee between her breasts. Keep to the subject at hand, he told himself.

"We aren't talking anatomy here, Nona," he said, perhaps sounding too longing. "We're arguing the basic character traits of male and female. The male is naturally aggressive, possessive of what he believes are his territorial rights. So..."

In spite of his tongue-in-cheek playing, Nicholas believed every word he was saying. It was possessiveness he felt as he looked at Nona. He wanted her next to him, his arms around her. When they had talked last night about her dating, he had felt a jealous twinge. He was already thinking in terms of *his* woman.

"So? What else were you going to say about the nature of females?" she asked feistily.

Jerked from his thoughts, Nicholas discovered himself confronting one testy lady. "So...uh...since females, by nature, lack aggressiveness, they have to learn it. So Tracy needs to be taught to be aggressive."

"You don't believe that."

Nicholas attempted to sound dour. "I believe it. Yes, I do. Moreover, I think as a rule, women are aggressive only when a man is involved."

"Pooh," Nona said disdainfully. "In my opinion a woman is only aggressive or assertive when her child needs defending."

"Pooh, yourself, Nona Alexander." Her eyes were snapping. He felt himself starting to laugh, and cleared his throat. "I hold onto my original statement. A woman is passive by nature. It takes a man to bring out the aggressiveness."

"And I still say pooh," Nona insisted.

"I don't suppose you'd like to put this to the test— you and me in a little game of one-on-one," he said. He was dying to get her into a game of one-on-one, but he wasn't thinking basketball.

"You want to test me to see how aggressive I can be?" Nona asked slowly. Suddenly she wondered if they were talking basketball...or some other, more stimulating kind of one-on-one.

"I am. Set the time and place."

"Wednesday. Beaver Crossing gym. Right after my girls practice. Say, six?"

"I usually visit the nursing home on Wednesday and eat dinner there."

She scoffed, "I knew you wouldn't do it."

"I'll pass up dinner. You've got a date, lady."

"Bring your own bandages!"

Their laughter finally burst, and Nona choked out, "Skiing is one thing, Nicholas, but I really would have beaten you if we had gone one-on-one."

"What do you mean really would have if we had?" Nicholas asked. "You accepted the challenge."

"Oh, Nicholas! I was teasing."

"Oh, Nona! I wasn't." He shifted. "I gather you're thinking about how it would look."

"Yes," Nona said, sighing.

"*Are* we going to be seeing each other?"

"Yes," she conceded, knowing she could perhaps deny him but she couldn't deny herself.

"We're not going to sneak around. Our relationship is honest. We've no reason to hide." He walked across the room to stand before her, his hand extended. "Come with me."

And be my love, his eyes seemed to say. Nona shook off the thought. It was insanity. "I...do have to be going," she said. But her hand was in his. He didn't so much pull her to standing as his gaze lured her to her feet.

His hands were on her forearms. The trembling, the warmth, the aching, all started again. She reiterated, "I have to be going."

"I know you have your classes to prepare for," he said, his voice sounding gravelly. He dropped his hands. "But I have something for you. It's in my study in the church. It will only take a minute."

He led the way. As they passed the den where Ivy was sitting at a desk, Nona stuck her head through the door. "Thank you, Ivy."

"I enjoyed your company, Nona," Ivy said. "Do come again. It's been a long time since I had the girl giggles."

"What were the two of you giggling about when I walked in before lunch?" Nicholas asked as they continued down the hall.

"It wouldn't be funny if I told you."

"You were talking about me, weren't you?" Nicholas asked.

"Of course we were talking about you," Nona said. "What else do we have in common we'd consider funny?"

Nicholas took her coat from the closet, smelled her perfume on it, then on her body as he held the coat for her. Did thoughts about him consume her time as thoughts about her consume his, he wondered.

He ran his fingers through her hair slowly, lifted it free of the coat collar, whispered in her ear, "I'm glad you were talking about me, Nona."

Nicholas opened the church door and held it, allowing Nona to step inside.

"I suppose you've been here before," Nicholas stated.

"Yes," Nona said. "Every fall for the Harvest Supper. And Mother and I came to Reverend Lockhart's retirement party."

They were standing in a long hall. At the end of it was a window. Golden sunlight shimmered on the oak floor. The quiet was profound.

"I forgot about that," Nicholas said. "That's where you met Adeline Drew."

The feeling of foreboding crept over Nona again. "I know you believe in the basic good of people, but watch out for her, will you?"

"I appreciate your concern, but don't worry about it," he said. He took her arm. "Now before I give you what I have for you, I want to show you something else. A first for me in Oak Valley."

He led her to the Sunday school room, to a scroll hanging on the wall. "This is the Cradle Roll membership." He pointed to the last name. "Our newest member is Harrington Granville, baptized last Sunday." He chuckled. "Harrington was sleeping soundly in his mother's arms when I woke him. He objected vociferously, much to his parents' embarrassment."

Nicholas sounded wistful. She's seen him with Kelly, members of his youth group and the high-school students he refereed. It was not difficult for Nona to deduce his yearning to have a child.

"You didn't mind, did you," she stated.

"In my opinion children enhance not only the quality of life, but the quality of a worship service," he said thoughtfully, smiling.

"I agree," Nona said. "In fact I love the children's sermons." She grinned. "Because I understand them."

"The truth be known, that's why we ministers have children's sermons, so the adults will get the point."

THE PERFECT WIFE

"I'd always suspected as much," Nona said drolly. "Do you and Ivy have other sisters and brothers?" she asked.

"There were three of us," he said, his eyes growing sorrowful. "But my brother, Tim, five years younger than I, died at eight months. Crib death."

"You remember him well, don't you?" Nona asked.

"I do. I suppose that's why I always liked babies when I was a kid. Ivy took baby-sitting jobs. Nine times out of ten, she found an excuse to have me fill in for her. I never let her know how much I liked it."

"How much of her wages did you keep?"

"All of it," he said, laughing. "I always wanted—" He took Nona's arm. "What I have for you is in my study."

Nona had seen the flash of despair in his eyes. He'd been about to say he had always wanted children. She wanted to ask why he and Corinne hadn't had a family, but if he'd wanted her to know, he'd have told her.

He opened the study door.

"Have a chair. What I want to give you is right here in my desk drawer."

"I'm getting more and more curious," Nona said. She sat, and Nicholas settled on his swivel chair behind the large desk.

"Don't build your hopes too high. This isn't an art treasure," he said, grinning.

Behind him, the wall was lined with book shelves, all filled. On another wall, there was an artful arrangement of pictures. On another, a stone fireplace with a Seth Thomas clock on the mantel. There was a sofa with throw pillows before the fireplace, and a vase filled with strawflowers. The colors here were earthy. The study was Nicholas—vital, masculine, solid.

But again, no picture of Corinne. And that struck Nona as strange. Then maybe not. It could be that pictures were too painful a reminder. When Nona's gaze came back to Nicholas, he placed a sheet of heavy white paper on the desk. "A sketch you've drawn?" she guessed.

"A sketch I've drawn." He slid the work to Nona.

It was a pencil sketch of the violet. The detail of the flower itself made her want to touch it. The log looked as real and lay exactly as she remembered it. He had even captured the shadowy indentations in the snow where first she, then he, had knelt to look at the plant.

She looked up. "When I asked if you were good at drawing and you said yes, you were right. And this is a treasure." She shook her head as if perplexed. "Next, I suppose, you'll tell me you write poetry," she said, teasing but believing he might.

"No poetry," he said.

He was gregarious, sensitive, fun-loving...and suffering a deeply troubling grief. At the moment, Nona didn't know what he was thinking, but she was thinking he hadn't kissed her all day and she wanted to be kissed.

She quickly decided she had better leave before she threw herself into his arms. That would hardly be the type of conduct one would expect from a friend.

"And the picture is mine to keep." she stated.

"I was thinking of you when I drew it," he said.

The now familiar speeding up of her heart hit her; she felt the tingling of warmth all over. Telling herself that it's because she was wearing her coat didn't help. She knew why she was warm, who her heart was beating for.

Her pragmatic approach to life was giving way to the mystery, the magic, the sweetness of falling in love.

"Then I'm taking my picture and going home," she said, faking lighthearted exuberance. "Thank you, Nicholas. It's lovely."

Nona and Mel were talking at center court after having dismissed the girls from practice when Mel's gaze went to the gymnasium door.

"I've got a question for you," Mel said. "What's tall, dark-haired, wears sweats and is holding a basketball?"

"Oh, no," Nona moaned. She turned slowly toward the door.

Nicholas was surrounded by her girls and some players from the boys' team who had arrived early for their practice at seven. They looked her way, laughed or giggled.

Well, Nona thought angrily. He wanted it, whatever *it* was, in the open. And it sure as heck was in the open now. "I really didn't think he would come," she stammered. "I thought he was teasing."

"Do I dare ask about what?" Mel asked.

Without taking her gaze from Nicholas, Nona explained about their one-on-one. Milly and William had appeared and joined the group around Nicholas.

"I think a short game against the boys would be a good thing for the girls. They could stand a little toughening up. And it appears enough boys are here," Mel said.

"Don't—" Nona said, but he had already walked away. Moments later, he had appointed Missy as girls' captain and William as boys' captain, designated himself as referee and told Milly to man the scoreboard.

Nona, bemused, found herself in the game with Nicholas. He had stripped off his sweats, revealing red shorts and jersey. His legs were long, still wearing a Texas tan. She thought a minister should *not* have legs that looked that good.

Mel had told everyone Nicholas had challenged her one-on-one, so they were going to kill two birds with one stone: scrimmaging and going man-to-man, or girl-to-boy, or man-to-woman. At that point, Mel had knocked off the descriptions because she'd given him a look which told him she could happily have thrown a stone or two at him.

Play commenced.

"This is going to be interesting," Nicholas whispered in her ear.

"Stop that," she whispered back.

"Stop what?"

"You're breathing in my ear."

"I didn't intend to breath in your ear but it isn't a bad idea because the objective is to distract the opponent any way you can."

"Stop that!"

"Loosen up, Nona. This is just an old-fashioned scrimmage between the sexes."

"You aren't funny. I don't like the fact that you deliberately ignored how I felt about this," she snapped.

"I didn't ignore how you felt. I can only tell you this is important to me. We have nothing to hide. Our relationship is honest. Open to scrutiny by anyone."

"It certainly will be after today!"

"Am I still your buddy?"

Nona could only growl in response. Cara passed her the ball, and after executing complex maneuvers to break away from Nicholas, she threw it to Kate, who shot and sank it.

As the girls yelled in triumph, Nona called, "Tracy. See what I did?"

Tracy nodded.

Nona batted her lashes at Nicholas. "The weaker sex strikes, not with aggressiveness but with finesse."

"Finesse, your foot, my pretty lady. I wasn't ready for action or you'd never have gotten that pass by me."

"Oh, really?" Nona asked.

She had the ball again and was facing Nicholas. She taunted him. "Okay? Are you ready?"

He slapped at the ball. The girls screamed, "Foul! Foul!" The boys catcalled. Nona made it to the basket and sprang. But Nicholas had jumped with her, ready to block her shot.

Still airborne, she twisted and managed to get the ball away. To her surprise and great pleasure, she sank the shot.

The girls whooped and hollered. The boys yelled, "Lucky shot!"

Nona and Nicholas were left standing alone again, watching the play in the opposite court.

"You're good," Nicholas said.

"Hmm," Nona responded to the caressing tone of his voice. "I am on to you, Nicholas Kendrick. You can't beat me fair and square so you're cheating by trying to distract me!"

She saw William shove Tracy and called, "Tracy! Don't allow William to do that to you. Get tough! Hold your ground!"

"Uh-oh," Nicholas whispered. "Look at Tracy's face. I think she's just realized what this game is about."

For the next fifteen minutes, both expended their energy competitively. Mel, walking past her said in a low voice, "Looks like a war, Nona. Looks like a war."

It was a war, Nona agreed. She was battling herself. On the one hand was her need to be with Nicholas anywhere, anyhow. On the other hand was the knowledge that while Nicholas needed her now to distract himself from thinking about Corinne, he wouldn't always need her. But by that time she might still need him....

"I was right, wasn't I?" Nicholas asked. The game was over, the girls had gone to the showers. The boys had gathered around their coach, who had been watching the action from the sidelines. Nicholas wiped his brow. "Males bring out the tigress in the gentle sex."

Nona was still panting. "Only when the tiger tries to shove his superior weight around."

"I am amazed," Nicholas said drolly. "You're a sore loser."

"I did not lose. And you know it," Nona said.

"I didn't either," Nicholas said. "Are you going to invite me to your place for coffee and conversation?"

"No," Nona said. When a flash of hurt registered in his eyes, she heard herself asking, "Do you like chili?"

"Love it."

"Would you like to come to dinner? Mother is waiting for Milly and me."

"Love to."

She wished he'd stop using *that* word. "I'll be showered in fifteen minutes." She glanced around. "Guess Milly's already gone. Uh, I could give you the directions to our house."

"Are you walking?"

"Yes."

"I'll be showered in ten. And waiting to drive you."

"It's only two blocks."

"Shall we walk?"

Walk alone with him along the quiet streets of Beaver Crossing with the snow crunching beneath their feet? And if he slipped his arm around her—for warmth—she might be tempted to cuddle...

"No. Since you have your car, I might as well ride."

She smiled, then nearly ran for the locker room. Way to go, Nona, she told herself. That was real control. She knew she was tempting fate every time she was with him. And she had invited him to dinner!

Chapter Nine

The wind had picked up while they ate dinner, but the fire crackling in the fireplace made the room feel snug and secure, Nicholas reflected.

No. The feeling of comfort came because he was alone with Nona, sharing the davenport with her. She was sitting slightly forward, her elbows on her knees, holding a cup of coffee. The fire cast an umber glow in her hair, and the atmosphere warmed even more for Nicholas.

"I had a good time tonight," he said. "Are you still mad at me?"

Her gaze slowly came around to him. "I should be furious but I'm not. I guess the bottom line is that you have more at risk than I do. And since it's your neck—" she hesitated when he ran his fingers up her neck and toyed with the curve of her jaw "—on the line. You made the call."

"You didn't say if it was fun," he prodded. He savored the feel of her, the way she responded to him, her eyes softening in anticipation.

She playfully shook his hand away. "Yes. It was fun."

"And educational," he added. "Even during our battle of the sexes, you were instructing Tracy. Teaching is an integral part of what makes you happy, isn't it?"

Nona smiled. "Once I would have answered that with an unequivocal yes. Now I know teaching is just one of the things intrinsic to my happiness, not the only thing."

She shifted to look at him more directly. "But I'm dealing with a job. I consider it a profession. How do you view being a minister?"

"Are you asking if I had a calling?"

"I thought in this case vocation and calling were synonymous," Nona said.

"I believe it is, too," Nicholas agreed. "But I'm not one of those ministers who professes he's spoken with God." He placed his cup on the coffee table. "My calling was something I felt in my heart. I was sure that this was the way I had to live my life."

Nona nodded and smiled as she considered what he'd said. "Now I understand what you were saying Saturday night. You might doubt yourself, but never your faith because your faith is felt so deeply, it can't be questioned."

"Good grief," Nicholas said. He chuckled a bit nervously. "Did I say that?"

Nona straightened. "Don't fence with me, Nicholas. Not on important issues."

He threw his hands up in a gesture of submission. "Okay. No fencing on important issues. The doubts I've had about my ministry are at a conscious level," he said. "They originate in my mind. I have never lost my faith in God or questioned his reality. I've only questioned my right to minister."

"Frankly, Nicholas, I don't understand why you question your right to minister," Nona said emphatically.

Nicholas took the cup from her hand and set it down. When he leaned back, he drew Nona with him, leaving his arm over her shoulder.

"This is better," he said, avoiding her probing comment.

She nestled her head. "Better."

Nicholas touched his lips to her temple and swam lazily in a warm current of desire. "I have to tell you I like you even better without makeup, fresh from the shower and soapy smelling," Nicholas said.

She looked up. Her eyes were luminous, filled with desire. Nicholas shuddered.

"You're crazy," she whispered.

"You're a great sounding board."

"You're... making suggestions," she stammered.

"I haven't said a word," he whispered, nuzzling her hair. She smelled so sweet.

"I read it in your eyes."

"Yes, you did," he said, seeking her lips.

She escaped him. "I see you've finished your coffee. Care for another cup?" She leaned forward as if prepared to go for it.

Nicholas drew her back, keeping his arm between her and the sofa. "Thank you, but no. I've been drinking too much coffee lately. We did bargain for a kiss, didn't we?"

"Me, too," Nona said. "I keep telling myself to cut down or stop drinking it all together. But I guess I'm just too weak-willed to resist the temptation. We settled on an occasional kiss."

He splayed his fingers in the middle of Nona's back, ran his fingers up and down her backbone. "You aren't weak-willed," he said.

Nona had always believed she was strong-willed, independent. But what about the temptation he presented? The same logic that told her too much caffeine was bad for her heart, told her that seeing too much of him would have the same result.

On the other hand she liked the feel of his fingers working her spine. And his teasing touch was very...

"You're right," she said, trying to snap herself out of her sensual lethargy. "I'm not weak-willed. I must be addicted to caffeine."

He slipped his hand up to her shoulder and tugged her close. "I like watching you talk."

Nona's lashes fluttered closed. She was thinking about paradise. "Don't you mean you like listening to me talk?"

"I like that, too. Your voice is evocative. A husky contralto that keeps surprising me. But watching your lips move..."

He was breathing the words past her ear as he ran his fingers over her lips, her cheek and her lashes. She shivered and felt his body respond with a tremor.

This was more than she had bargained for. "T-Tracy," she stammered, "will never be the same after tonight."

"I will never be the same after tonight."

Nona wouldn't open her eyes. She *couldn't* open her eyes. She was lost now. If she met his gaze she would be lost forever.

"I got a little carried away at the game," she said.

"I'm getting a little carried away myself. I'm leaving as soon as you answer the question."

Nona's eyes opened in alarm. "I didn't hear a question."

"For the last five minutes I've been asking it. But the question isn't important. Just say yes!"

"Yes?" she asked.

"No. Say yes!"

"Yes?"

"You still don't have it quite right. Like this. With no lingering doubts, with enthusiasm—yes!"

"Yes!"

"That's what I've been waiting to hear," Nicholas said.

He settled his lips on hers. This time there was no hesitation on his part, no slow familiarizing. And he felt no hesitation on her part. His body came to life when she melted to him, exploring his face with her fingertips.

He cradled her silky head and kissed her deeply. His fingers traveled down her neck, picking up the texture of her skin—silk again. He sighed when he caressed the soft curves of her breasts. He slid down on the sofa, taking her with him.

He felt her draw in her breath and not release it. With a start, he realized what he was doing. He slowly eased them up. This needed more thought, more consideration. Not because he didn't know what he was feeling for Nona—he knew—but he had to know if he was capable of loving Nona the way she deserved to be loved.

"This needs more thought, Nona. I'm moving too fast." He kissed her lips, her chin. "I'm going to get out of here." He pushed her away.

Surprise didn't describe what Nona felt. She wasn't sure rejection did, either. But as she studied the worried expression on his face, she felt that at some point in kissing her, he had thought about Corinne and realized what he felt for her paled in comparison to what he had felt for his wife.

He reached for his jacket, which lay over the back of the sofa, stood and slipped it on. Nona picked up their cups and stood. His hair was tousled, tumbling down to his brows and giving him a childish, bewildered appearance. She put down the urge to straighten his hair, touch his furrowed brow.

He kissed her on the cheek. "When do I see you next?"

"Whenever you feel you need a sounding board, I guess."

After a long, probing look, he nodded and left the house. Nona sank to the sofa and stared into the fire. The man had rattled the cocoon of security she had woven around herself. Happiness was not a thing of the past, she assured herself. But she acknowledged a tug of discontent with the way she had been living her life.

A week later, on the first day of Christmas vacation, Nona was placing the last decorations on the Christmas tree when the doorbell rang. She paused for a moment to admire the tree before going to open the door.

"Nona Alexander?" the man asked.

"Yes."

He handed her a long white florist's box tied with a red ribbon and bow. "Merry Christmas."

"Merry Christmas. And thank you," Nona said.

She closed the door, walked to the sofa and sat. Nicholas? she wondered as she opened the box. She pulled the tissue aside to reveal a single yellow rose. She lifted the card.

"This flower pales in comparison to the flower I discovered in the timber. Nicholas."

She smelled the rose. Its scent was heady. She knew she would never again smell the aroma of a rose without thinking about Nicholas. Or see a violet without thinking about Nicholas. Or hear a deep-throated laugh...

It was because of him she had called Jon, Sr. and Emily, and last night had driven down to visit them. After their initial discomfort, the barriers had broken and she had discovered why they had seemed distant during her previous visit.

Jon had told them about Joann before he had told her. They admitted they had wanted to tell her, and to do something to make Jon look at what he was doing. But they had ended up doing nothing and had felt guilty about it.

Because of Nicholas, a weight she had been carrying was lifted. In big and small ways, he was changing the fabric of her life, but he hadn't called. And she'd told him when he needed a sounding board—or an occasional kiss—she'd be available.

So she shouldn't call him now. she neither wanted to push, or be pushed. A little thank-you note would do, she decided as she walked into the kitchen. A thank-you note was exactly the right thing, she reasserted as she searched for and found a vase, drew water, and put the rose in.

She walked to the telephone and dialed the parsonage. It's no big deal if I just talk to him, she told herself.

"Kendrick residence. Ivy Kipling speaking."

Ivy sounded hurried. Or harassed, Nona thought. "Ivy, this is Nona," she said.

They exchanged pleasantries, then Nona inquired, "You sound hurried, Ivy. Did I call at a bad time?"

"Not really. I'm just getting ready for a Ladies' Aid meeting. They're planning a bake sale and luncheon," Ivy said.

"More cookies and salad," Nona stated.

"Sounds like," Ivy agreed, sighing.

They visited congenially for a few minutes, then Nona asked if Nicholas was available.

"He's taken a van load of elderly people Christmas shopping in Sioux City. They're going to stop at the hospital to see Ralph. Agnes was released yesterday."

"That's good to hear."

"Will you be home later this afternoon? He could call you then?"

"I have a basketball practice at two."

"How about after supper?" Ivy suggested helpfully.

"I'll be at church until about ten. We're getting ready for the Christmas Eve program. I'll call another time," Nona said.

"I just remembered Nicholas has a confirmation class tonight," Ivy said. "You two are busy people."

After Nona hung up, she studied the rose. Nicholas's days were filled. Hers were filled. Occasional didn't mean weekly. It meant occasionally.

What did she want from Nicholas? She touched the rose, felt him, his tenderness, his thoughtfulness. But how many times did she have to come face-to-face with reality? By nature and disposition, she wasn't the kind of person who liked Ladies' Aid meetings. Or baked cookies for a bake sale or attended luncheons. She even skipped church occasionally.

He had said he was moving too fast? Her eyes misted. She was light-years ahead of him. She was already thinking of a minister's wife's duties—and headed for disaster. He said it needed more thought. And it did.

After Nona got home from church, she started cleaning a kitchen cupboard. She knew Ivy would tell

Nicholas she'd called and she knew him well enough to know that he would be calling as soon as he was free.

When the phone rang at ten-thirty, she smiled and picked the handset up on the second ring.

"Nona speaking."

"Where's your answering service?"

"Playing bingo at a competitive church."

Nicholas laughed. "You're going to have to fire her. Recover from the scrimmage, yet?"

"No. Not really," Nona said. "You were no gentleman."

"I still have an achy back."

"Poor baby." Nona mimicked his croon.

"I know it's late, but why don't I drive up so you can rub my back?"

Nona carried the phone across the kitchen and looked out the window. Thank him for the gift and get it over with, she told herself. "Thank you for the rose, Nicholas. I've never had so thoughtful a Christmas gift."

"I take it that was a no to rubbing my back?"

Nona could see to the corner from the kitchen window. Under the light, two young people stood with their arms around each other, occasionally kissing, occasionally talking.

Nona turned from the window and sat on a chair. "I'm tempted to tell you to come by, but I do think you're right. We're moving too fast. I've been thinking...maybe we ought to limit occasionally to say...once a month."

"Give me a break, Nona," Nicholas said slowly. "Things got a little out of hand. But once a month?"

"It wasn't that much out of hand," Nona said, forcing lightness into her tone. "I didn't twist your arm, did I? Maybe... a couple of times a month."

"A *couple* of times?"

When Nona didn't answer, he said. "The rose was a to-let-you-know-I've-been-thinking-about-you kind of gift, Nona, because I was thinking of you even though I couldn't break free. I did call three times. You were gone. Jenny didn't even answer."

"She was visiting Lillian in Des Moines. Maybe once a week," Nona said.

She had spoken casually, but she'd heard the loneliness in her voice. Whatever she'd been doing, whomever she'd been with, she'd been lonely. Lonely for Nicholas because he had become necessary to her contentment.

"Tomorrow night. Around eight?" he asked abruptly.

"I don't know—"

"I've been thinking along the line of sharing the sofa with you, watching you watch the fire burn. I won't push, not until we're both ready."

Nona sank to a chair, resigned. So much for willpower, self-discipline and all the other stuff she'd always had pride in having. "All right. Tomorrow night."

They were still on the phone when Jenny walked into the kitchen an hour later. Still talking when Jenny went to bed.

Before their conversation ended, they had committed to seeing each other the following night and the day after when they would go to Sioux City to do some Christmas shopping.

Nona had also accepted his invitation to go caroling with his church youth group. He had arranged for the use of a team of horses to pull a hayrack around Oak Valley.

They had admitted that the most important thing between them was their friendship. And while neither had expressed it, the undertone of the conversation clearly stated that they were going to keep it cool, fun, light-hearted.

"I thought we came to the mall to Christmas shop for your five nephews and nieces and Kelly," Nicholas said.

"Give me just a minute more," Nona said. "Aren't these Shelties the cutest dogs you've ever seen!"

For the last ten minutes, Nona had stood in front of the windows of the pet store, moving from the puppies to the pug-nosed kittens and back to the dogs.

She was demonstrating the same kind of uninhibited exuberance she'd shown the night of the boxing match. Her mood permeated the air. He was the happiest he'd been in years. She was, perhaps, the best friend he'd ever had, male or female.

"They're cute," Nicholas said. "Now can we go?"

"What are you? A nervous shopper?" she asked as she turned from the window.

"I don't call waiting around for ten minutes nervous."

Nona tossed him an oh-really look. "Someday I'm going to buy a few acres," she said. "Build a kennel and raise collies."

She hooked her arm through his. "Come on. Let's move it. Time is a-wasting as they say."

Nicholas laughed. They joined the heavy stream of shoppers.

"So who takes care of the kennel?" he asked. "Or is someday like after you retire from teaching when you're sixty or seventy?"

"Don't worry about it. When it happens, it happens. Maybe next year." She frowned mischievously. "Or when I'm seventy. I'll handle it."

"And what if... in the future, you end up marrying a man who doesn't like dogs. What then?" Nicholas asked.

She shrugged her coat off. Nicholas took it from her. "I'll carry it," he offered.

"Thank you," Nona said. "I'll carry it myself when you start carrying the packages."

"Very generous of you." They shared a smile and continued on, with Nona leading the way since she was familiar with the stores. "You never answered," Nicholas said. "What if you marry a man who doesn't like dogs?"

Her smile was patient. "*If* I ever marry again, I would never marry a man who didn't like dogs. I want to have lots of them. And children. Two at least. That's all there is to it."

"I like children," Nicholas said.

"Yes, I know," she said so softly that he didn't know if she'd actually spoken the words.

"And I like dogs," he stated firmly.

"That's nice," she said.

"And I like to be petted—"

She jabbed him lightly in the ribs. But beneath the bantering, she was having sober thoughts. She had begun to wonder if marriage was in her future. How could another man understand her as Nicholas did?

They found a toy store and fought the crowd to walk up one aisle and down another. "Do you have any idea what you're looking for?" Nicholas asked. Did she really know exactly what she wanted in a man?

Nona knew what she was looking for—and had found it in Nicholas. But it wasn't to be.... "Not in the slightest," she said. "But I'll know it when I see it. How about you? What are you getting Kelly?"

"Ice skates."

"Good choice. I have this prejudice against roller skates," Nona said.

They looked at each other and laughed.

Two hours later, they had purchased the ice skates and four of the five gifts Nona needed.

Nicholas, carrying the packages, grunted as he lifted his arm to check his watch. "We're running out of time, Nona. The stores are going to close before long."

"I know. But *I* wasn't the one who played with every toy *I* purchased to make sure it worked," she said, eyeing him meaningfully.

"You can't just rush up and buy a toy. You've got to test it," Nicholas said.

Nona stopped in her tracks and shook an accusing finger at him. "What about the Tinkertoys? Really. You see one Tinker toy and you've seen them all."

Her eyes were merry as the Christmas music being played in the mall. Nicholas shrugged. "There were different-sized sets you had to consider," he observed.

"Because you've wasted so much time playing with toys, if I don't find something for my nephew, Jess, in this store, I'm going to have to make another trip down. We go left here," she said, grabbing his arm and guiding him.

"Do I get to come shopping with you if you have to come again?" Nicholas asked.

"You've got to be kidding."

They had no more than entered the store when Nona stalled again. This time before a wall of stuffed animals. She picked up a cat with orange-and-black stripes and wearing a baseball hat and glove.

"Thinking of getting that for Jess?" Nicholas asked.

"Heavens, no. Jess is only six months old. But isn't this the cutest thing you've ever seen?"

"Cuter than the dogs?"

"This is a different kind of cute."

Nicholas moved to the side to allow a man and woman pushing a cart loaded with toys to pass. "What do you do with a fat orange cat wearing a baseball hat?" he asked after they had moved on.

"Do with it?" Nona turned the cat over. "See these suction cups? You stick it on the window of your car—"

Nicholas broke up.

"I don't care what you think," she said, snickering. "It's cute!"

"You mean to tell me, you'd drive your station wagon around with *that* hanging in the window?"

"Of course I would," Nona said. She moved toward a display of crib mobiles.

Nicholas wandered to the display of trains, then watched a little windup train circle a small track. It reminded him of the first train he'd ever had.

"Nona! Come here," he called.

Nona came from where she had been looking at the stuffed toys again. "The sign says, DO NOT TOUCH," she said with mock sternness. "And that means you, Nicholas."

"How could I touch anything, even you?" he asked. And he had been wanting to touch her, or lay his arm over her shoulder as they strolled through the mall. "I'm holding all the packages. But I wanted you to see this. Look at it belch smoke. Now that's cute!"

"Yes. It's cute," Nona said. "I didn't find anything for Jess. I'm starved. How about a hot dog?"

"Sounds good. Be right with you."

"You can't stand here all night watching that train go around and around and around the track."

"It's got to run down sometime. Maybe I'll buy it and set it on my desk."

"For heaven's sake!"

"Don't be impatient, Nona. I waited for you to get tired of watching the dogs, now you can wait for me to get tired of watching the train—"

"Go around and around and—"

"All right," Nicholas said. He laughed. "Lead me to the hot dogs."

* * *

The team of horses, their harnesses trimmed with bells, pulled the hayrack through the streets of Oak Valley. To the jingle of the bells and the plod of hooves, voices caroled in the still, moonlit night.

"Joy to the world," Nona sang.

She glanced over at Nicholas. Over the last week and a half, besides sitting around her place and his doing nothing, they had gone cross-country skiing, attended a piano recital one of his parishioners presented, distributed pantry goods to families in his congregation and exchanged Christmas presents.

Nona had made a dash to Sioux City to purchase the little train for Nicholas. He had made a dash of his own. Her station wagon was now the proud owner of a cat wearing a baseball hat, much to the amusement of the kids around town.

The gift exchange had been exactly right for a blossoming friendship. Not too personal but personal enough. They were in what Nona was calling a comfort zone.

They enjoyed being with each other. They avoided tense moments. Those they couldn't avoid, they eased away from with laughter.

They laughed quite often.

Nicholas sang, glancing at Nona.

As they were pulled slowly from one corner to another, families came to the windows, shoved aside the curtains and went to stand on their porches and join the singing.

Nona's face was beaming and Nicholas's joy shifted into overdrive. He leaned toward her. "Is this a perfect moment?"

"So perfect I keep looking for the angels to appear," she agreed.

Ivy, sitting on the far side of Nona, raised her gloved hand to her eyes and wiped a tear away.

"Ivy," Nona asked in a low voice, "are you all right?"

"It's just the time of year. The singing," Ivy whispered. "And I was thinking about Corinne. She had a lovely voice. She loved singing in the choir."

Nicholas winced inwardly. His jaw tightened in determination. Maybe he was selfish, uncaring—all the things he shouldn't be—but he wasn't going to allow Corinne's memory to drape over the evening like a shroud. It was going to remain a perfect evening. A night to remember and savor in years to come.

He ignored Ivy's comment.

"Merry Christmas, Nona," he said.

"And a joyous one to you, Nicholas."

It was the happiest one he had ever had. Since meeting Nona, he had never laughed so much, accomplished so much, felt so good about himself. He had been granted a rare gift—her presence.

"I'm looking forward to the new year," he said.

In the pale light, her eyes reflected thoughtfulness. He touched her cheek with his gloved fingers. He was coming ever closer to loving this woman. Each moment, ever closer.

"My life has renewed meaning because of you, Nona. It's because of your friendship that I'm looking forward to the coming year," he said.

"I'm glad, Nicholas. Very glad," she whispered.

Chapter Ten

Once Nicholas had told Nona that because of her friendship he was looking forward to the future, she stopped questioning her role in the relationship and adopted a wait-and-see attitude.

The days of December drifted into January and then February. When she made plans to treat her basketball team to a chili dinner at the conclusion of the season, she invited Nicholas. He had had a great deal to do with the team's success. First with Kate, then with Tracy, who had developed into a fine player once she had gained confidence in herself. The team had ended the season with a twelve-and-six record.

Nona was in the kitchen, stirring a huge kettle of chili when she heard her mother greet Nicholas. A moment later, he pushed open the swinging door of the kitchen and strolled in.

He grabbed a carrot stick from the relish tray as he passed the counter. Her reaction to him hadn't changed in three months—a little catch in her breathing, her heart speeding, a delightful tingling...

"If you were a child, I'd remind you that you'll spoil your appetite for dinner if you snack beforehand."

Nicholas finished the carrot and grinned. "Do kisses taken before dinner spoil an appetite?" he asked, leaning toward her.

His kiss was almost casual. It rendered Nona blissfully carefree. When he lifted his lips from hers, she said breathlessly, "You didn't give me a chance to answer."

"Didn't need your opinion. Your kisses are good for me."

He kissed her again.

Nona took a deep breath. "You're a guest. What are you doing in the kitchen?"

Nicholas wondered if Nona understood yet how much he loved her. If she didn't, she would. He would tell her that her name was in every breath he took, his arms felt empty when she wasn't in his embrace. "Jenny sent me to help you while she prepares to greet the dinner guests. I think she's trying to nudge the romance along," he said lightly.

"Romance!" Nona exclaimed. "Did she say that?"

He kissed the tip of her nose. Then her lips again before running the tip of his tongue over his lips. "You're spicy, Nona. 'Fess up. You've been tasting the chili."

"You caught me." She kissed him quickly. "I think you're spicy yourself, Nicholas Kendrick."

"Your mother didn't use the word romance. I used it."

"Pooh," she said. "We're keeping company. I'm your sounding board."

"You certainly are, but I think there's more going on here than keeping company," Nicholas said. He leaned against the counter and folded his arms, feigning thoughtfulness. "Do you get a kind of tingling feeling when you see me?"

"Well...kind of...but I get a tingling feeling when I hear 'The Star Spangled Banner' played."

"I see," he said slowly. "Does your heart pound like crazy when you see me? I mean does it really do wild things."

"As a matter of fact, it does," Nona said and quickly added, "but my heart pounds before a basketball game, too. So you can see how confusing this is."

"It isn't confusing, at all. That tingling you feel when you see me, I feel it when I see you," he said. "It's excitement. And that thumping of your heart, I feel it, too." He raised her hand to his chest. "Am I lying?" he asked.

"No. Your heart is thumping," she whispered.

"That's anticipation," he said. "I think we've moved into a romance, don't you?"

She had fallen in love. No, she thought. She had loved him from the start. She hadn't wanted to admit it because loving him made the relationship so complicated. Loving him made her face herself, made her ask if she could be the kind of wife he needed.

She raised both hands to his face. She was familiar with the texture of his skin, the grainy feel when he needed a shave—and she knew he had to shave twice a day to achieve the smoothness she felt now, under her fingertips. "I—" A voice called, "Reverend Kendrick?"

"That's Kate," Nona said.

"In the kitchen," Nicholas yelled. He kissed Nona once more, then stepped away and was smiling toward the door when it was pushed open.

Kate, Cara, Missy and Tracy rushed into the kitchen.

"You didn't tell him, did you?" Kate asked.

"Of course not."

"Tell me what?" Nicholas asked.

"It just happened today, Reverend Kendrick. I was offered a basketball scholarship to the University. Mrs. Alexander took films of games, asked some other coaches for letters of recommendation and I got it. A scholarship!"

"Way to go, Kate," Nicholas said.

"Mrs. Alexander said you were the one who came up with the idea of the chair. I really don't know how to thank you because I couldn't have gone to college without the scholarship."

"You, Mrs. Alexander, Mr. Baldwin and the whole team did the hard work," Nicholas said.

Kate smiled at the other girls.

"I can hardly wait until next year," Tracy bubbled.

"You'd never guess by looking at this sweet face," Missy said, patting Tracy's cheek playfully, "that Tracy considers herself a giant-killer."

Tracy giggled. The girls broke into lively conversation. Nona and Nicholas looked at each other and grinned.

Milly, wearing black lounging pajamas with splashes of white, swept into the kitchen, pulling a tall, thin young man with her. "Everybody! Jim and I are here! Let's eat!"

Cara gushed, "Miss Brooks! Where did you get that outfit? I *love* it."

Mel and his wife had followed Milly into the kitchen. Mel gruffed, "Cara, for heaven's sake! Are you blind? That outfit makes Milly look like an escapee from an exotic zoo."

Milly, with great drama, collapsed against Jim. "Defend me, my hero, from this cruel man."

Jim shoved her away, laughing. "Defend yourself, Milly."

Milly glanced around. "Girls! You know a fashion plate when you see it? Don't you?"

As one, the girls took after Mel in defense of Milly. Mel asked for Nicholas's opinion.

"Milly's outfit...uh...it's nice," Nicholas said.

Mel exclaimed. "You do need glasses, Nicholas. Better get them before the basketball season starts next year."

Nona laughed with everyone else. Next year, she thought. Would they still be having a romance? Would they be seeing each other, at all?

Because if Nicholas was falling in love with her, then they would both have to ask themselves how she fitted into his life. What kind of wife would she make for a minister? The image of the perfect wife surfaced from Nona's memory. And she hadn't thought about Corinne in a long time....

Before her spirits could plummet, she called over the voices and laughter, "If I could get a word in. Would someone grab the crackers from the bread box? Call the rest of the gang from the front room. Soup's on!"

Where has the time gone? Nona wondered as she stood in line behind Emily and Jon Sr., waiting to visit briefly with Nicholas, who was shaking hands with members of the congregation as they left the church after the service.

She didn't know what had happened to time, but it was mid-May and she and Nicholas were still together, still comfortable with each other. The bonding Nicholas had spoken about was deepening.

Jon Sr. and Emily moved away. Nona stepped ahead, slipped her hand into Nicholas's. "Beautiful day, Reverend Kendrick."

"I'm so happy you were finally able to make it." He squeezed her hand. "What did you think of the sermon?"

On Saturday nights they often discussed his text for the following morning. They hadn't last night because when she had told him she was going to attend the service with the Alexanders, he'd grinned, then kissed her. "Good," he'd said. "You can hear the sermon for yourself. Tonight we can get on to the really important things." He'd kissed her again.

And right now she couldn't recall what he'd said. She'd gotten lost in the music of his voice, the movement of his hands and the expression on his face when the children gathered in front for their special sermon.

"Very interesting," she said in answer to his question.

"Interesting can either be good or bad," he suggested, smiling.

Nona eased her hand out of his. "You didn't bore me."

"The Alexanders said you were having lunch with them."

"I am," she said. She looked around for the Alexanders, located them visiting with Ivy and Mr. and Mrs. Timmons. Shivers of apprehension crawled up her spine when she saw Adeline Drew join them. "So I'd better go before they leave me."

Nicholas was smiling when she met his gaze, and in his eyes, she saw him saying, I'll see you tonight. She nodded and made her way to the Alexanders, hoping to arrive in time to hear what Adeline was saying.

At Emily's suggestion, she, Nona and Jon, Sr. took a walk to work off their just-finished lunch. They went briskly down the lane, which was bordered on one side by a corn field, on the other by a small pasture where three mares grazed with their foals.

Jon, Sr. grinned down at his wife. "That was a real feast, Emily," he said. "Nona, did I ever tell you

Emily didn't know how to cook when we got married?"

"You have. Also how everything she knows about cooking you taught her," Nona said. Jon, Sr. reminded her of Jon in looks.

"I did a fair job of it, too, if I do say so myself," Jon, Sr. said, teasing Emily with his eyes.

Emily, trim and strikingly pretty, laughed scoffingly. "Left on your own, Jon, you'd starve and you know it. The only thing you ever knew about food was how to pull your chair up to the table once the food was on. And since you can't break that habit, we have to walk."

"New health regimen?" Nona inquired.

"Ye gods, yes," Jon snorted. "The program committee of the Ladies' Aid was trying to line up their program, so Reverend Kendrick suggested this fitness nut might be willing to talk at a meeting."

Jon, Sr. continued, trying to sound gruff. "The next thing I knew Emily went to a meeting and came home talking oatmeal bread and two miles' walking a day. Some darn nonsense about cholesterol."

Emily gave Nona a tickled look. "Jon thinks Reverend Kendrick is a young whippersnapper."

Jon, Sr. grinned. Nona smiled. She knew the Alexanders liked Nicholas, but it was nice to hear.

Jon, Sr. wandered from the lane to the pasture fence. "Come take a closer look at these foals, Nona." He yelled for the horses. The mares trotted toward the fence. The foals frolicked along. For a few minutes Jon, Sr., Emily and Nona talked horses, rubbed velvet noses and laughed at the foals' antics.

When they were walking down the lane again, the horses followed along the fence. Nona glanced over her shoulder. "That black colt is a dandy," she observed.

"The last time Reverend Kendrick was here for a visit, he took a liking to him, too," Emily said. "I thought he made some good points in his sermon today, didn't you, Nona?" she added.

Nona smiled, then answered in a roundabout way, "If you think he made some good points, Emily, I won't disagree."

They had reached the end of the lane. Nona held back long enough to see the Alexanders had no intention of turning around. They walked south along the timber-shaded gravel road.

"Reverend Kendrick doesn't take an hour to make his points, either," Jon, Sr. said. He stuck his hands in his jeans pockets, shortened his stride to adjust to Emily's. He smiled, "No banging on the pulpit, just good, straight talk."

"That's high praise coming from you," Nona offered with a grin.

Emily chuckled. "Not only from Jon. Attendance at Sunday services has doubled," she offered.

Jon, Sr. grew thoughtful. "I'm afraid he won't be here long. One of the big churches will lure him away. The salary we can afford isn't all that good."

"Nicholas had a large church in Dallas. I don't think money is one of his priorities," Nona said.

Jon, Sr. smiled. "I hear you're getting to be." Nona paled. "I was teasing. We're happy you're seeing Reverend Kendrick."

"You deserve a chance at happiness," Emily asserted. She slipped her arm around Nona's waist, tugged her close, then released her.

"I know you were teasing, Jon. And I know you want me to be happy, but I gather there's been talk about Nicholas and myself," Nona said.

"You know how it is, dear," Emily said. "A few people like to talk. Usually it's about something they don't know anything about."

They came to a wooden bridge. In her preoccupation, Nona didn't realize for a moment the Alexanders had turned around. She looked back to discover the Alexanders wearing concerned expressions.

"I wish you'd tell me what you've heard," Nona said.

Jon, Sr. and Emily exchanged glances.

Jon, Sr. sighed. "Adeline Drew has expressed the opinion that Reverend Kendrick's spending too much time with you, which is out-and-out stupid," he said. "We've never had a minister who gave so much of himself to us as he does."

Nona frowned. When she had joined Mrs. Timmons, the Alexanders and Adeline after church, Adeline had seemed pleasant enough. She hadn't met Nona's gaze, but then the woman hadn't met her gaze that night at the hospital.

"Nicholas and I ran into Adeline at the hospital the night—"

Emily snapped, "I am so sick of hearing Adeline tell about seeing Reverend Kendrick kissing you, I could choke her."

Nona felt herself pale to her toes.

Emily's eyes flashed. She sputtered, "That woman is a real—"

"Not nice, Emily," Jon, Sr. suggested with a laugh.

"She's not nice, either," Emily snapped.

"It was a peck on the cheek," Nona said. They had turned back up the lane.

"For heaven's sake, Nona, people know that," Emily asserted. "Land! If you were having an affair, you'd sneak around."

"Adeline ought to sweep her own back steps before starting on someone else's," Jon, Sr. said quietly.

Nona stopped. The Alexanders turned to face her. "She's saying—" she was shaking "—we're having an affair?"

"Hell, no," Jon, Sr. nearly yelled. "Adeline doesn't have the guts to say it straight out so anyone can challenge her. She insinuates."

"Don't worry about it, Nona," Emily said quickly. "Adeline is a bitter woman who gets pleasure from making people unhappy. Her son, Tom, most of all. Everyone knows Adeline. No one pays any attention to her."

"I knew my dating Nicholas could have bad repercussions for him. I should have been smarter."

"You have a right to live the way you see fit," Jon, Sr. said firmly.

They walked again, Nona in the middle. Jon, Sr. and Emily linked arms with her in expression of their support. The conversation turned to the Alexanders' cattle-feeding operation. Nona tried to concentrate on what was being said.

Her world was tumbling end-over-end, out of control. She loved Nicholas so much. But the wait-to-see-what-would-happen time was over.

If dating her was going to jeopardize his standing in the community, be a threat to his ministry, her position as his friend, companion...romantic interest was untenable.

Nicholas shoved the porch swing slowly. Nona helped by giving an occasional push. "Someday," he said, "I'm going to have a porch swing. I think a man could get a lot of thinking done, sitting in a porch swing, smelling the night."

He slipped his arm over her shoulder. Nona smiled but moved away. "What's wrong, Nona? You've been edgy all night."

He reached for her hand. She patted his, then moved hers to her lap. "Okay," he said, "Let's hear it."

"I just don't think we should be holding hands. Someone might come down the street and see us. That's all."

"It's so dark I can barely see you and you're six inches away. How in the world is anyone going to see us from the street? And what difference is it going to make anyway?"

"I only feel that for the sake of appearances—"

"Not holding your hand will not make me not want to hold your hand," Nicholas said.

"I've...uh...been thinking maybe we should see less of each other."

"This is a new twist," Nicholas said. "What happened?"

"I think people have the idea we're...kind of a couple."

"We *are* a couple."

"No. We really *aren't* a couple. Not the way a few people think we're a couple," she said. "We're seeing each other because you were going through an emotional crisis. You needed companionship."

"The fact is, it was your companionship I needed."

"I happened to be available," she said.

Nicholas laughed. "That's not how I recall it. As I recall, you refused me the first time I asked you out."

"Because I knew our being together wasn't appropriate."

"Remember the day we discovered the violet blooming in the snow?" he asked.

"Of course I remember. The sketch is framed and hanging on my bedroom wall."

"I wonder what you'd done with it," he murmured. "I like knowing it's hanging there."

Nona shivered with the intimacy in his voice. "You were going to say something about the violet," she reminded him.

"That violet blooming in the snow was going against the laws of nature. It wasn't appropriate, either, was it?"

She nodded.

"But the flower was there," he continued, his voice growing more gentle, but powerfully intent. "It was a lovely surprise on a cold winter morning. It brightened my day, made me reflect on the gifts I'd been given."

Nona's breath caught when he touched her cheek, then trailed his finger to her lips and over them. "What's happening to us is surprising," he said. "It's a gift. But it's fragile at this point. Just as the violet was."

"So we can't walk away from our caring for each other like we did the violet, leave what we feel for each other to survive or die on its own. No matter how it might appear to others, we owe it to ourselves to nurture what we feel for each other to fruition."

Nona felt her resolve weakening. And if he'd said, "Nona I love you," she'd have fought Adeline Drew for the right to stand by his side. She would have said she knew she wasn't the kind of wife he needed, but she'd try. Still, he didn't say he loved her, and Nicholas was not a man who lacked for words. If he felt a special love for her, he'd have said it.

"I don't know how to argue against such beautiful sentiment, Nicholas," Nona said, sighing. "But the issue is whether or not it would be wise to nourish it. I can never be the kind of helpmate to you in your ministry that Corinne was."

He shocked her by laughing. "What kind of illogical thinking is that, Nona?" He took her hand and squeezed it. "You are all the helpmate any man could ever want."

"We aren't talking about any man," Nona said. Her hurt came out sounding defensive. "We're talking about the possibility of my becoming your wife."

"I was talking about that possibility, too," Nicholas said.

"Well..." Nona hesitated. "I'm not cut out to be a minister's wife. I have no patience for luncheons, leading choir practices, keeping a house spic-and-span, that kind of thing."

Nicholas sighed. Each time he tried to tell her he loved her, she seemed to sense it and throw up a barrier. And he didn't have the nerve to batter at the barrier because he couldn't risk driving her away, losing what they already had.

"Don't you think I know what I need in a wife?" he asked. "If I wanted another right hand, I'd look for one. What I need is a woman whose smile makes people feel loved. A woman who is unselfish in giving of herself."

Nona shook her head sadly. "I believe you believe what you're saying," she said slowly. "The problem is I don't believe it. There are still times when I feel you confuse me with Corinne."

His laugh was bittersweet. "Nona, nothing about you reminds me of Corinne. That first night—remember?"

"Of course I remember." Nona thought about the look.

"I gazed across the gym and saw a beautiful woman lifting Cara's chin. I didn't know what you were saying, but I knew by your gentleness you were giving her support."

Nicholas slipped his arm over her shoulder again, and this time Nona didn't object. She simply was dying. He still wasn't saying he loved her.

"Then I heard your gregarious laughter in response to something Mel said," he continued slowly. "And face to face what I saw were the most gorgeous blue eyes I'd ever seen. Eyes showing a generous, caring nature. A woman whose emotions were spontaneous, not contrived. Are you listening to me, Nona?"

"I'm listening," she said. And with each loving word he spoke, her love for him grew—and the more determined she became to protect him against himself. He was so naive!

"I thought I knew you. Now I know what I was feeling was how I wanted to know you," he said. "And we're getting to know each other, aren't we?"

"Yes," Nona agreed. "We're getting to know each other."

"So are we going to take care of what we have going?" he asked.

"With one part of my mind," she said slowly, "I want to continue to see you because I've grown to care very deeply about you. But with the logical, reasonable part, I think we should step back, not see each other for a while and think about it."

A heavy minute of silence fell between them. He stroked her shoulder. She held her breath. Finally, he said, "If you feel that strongly about it, I have no choice but to agree, do I?"

"No," Nona whispered.

"Would you agree on a deadline for the length of time we take to think about it?" he asked.

Nona nodded. She didn't trust herself to speak.

"The Ministerial Association is sponsoring a community picnic next Sunday," he said.

"I remember. You told me."

"Will that give you enough time to think things over?" he asked.

"Yes," Nona said. She wanted to cry. She needed to. But she was not going to. "Did I tell you I was leaving next Monday for a two-week seminar in Iowa City?" she asked. She knew she hadn't because until this very moment, she hadn't made up her mind.

"No, you didn't. What's the course study?"

"Physical conditioning, intensive training in first aid—"

"Nosebleeds?" he asked, touching her nose at the bridge. He ran his finger slowly down to the tip, then to her lips.

"I...would imagine it will include that topic," Nona whispered.

He drew her into his arms. "I need a kiss to hold me, Nona. Don't deny me that."

Chapter Eleven

Nicholas had just driven off and Nona was still sitting in the swing when the telephone rang.

She felt too dead to move. Her mother would get it. Then she remembered Jenny had walked over to visit Marsha. She flew into the house through the front room into the kitchen and grabbed the handset.

She took a deep breath. "Nona Alexander speaking."

"Nona. This is Ivy. Does Nicholas happen to be there?"

"He left about five minutes ago, Ivy."

"Good," Ivy said, sounding relieved. "Adeline Drew just called to say Tom had been admitted to a Sioux City hospital with chest pains. Tom wanted to see Nicholas."

"My goodness. I hope he'll be okay," Nona said. She had to ask, "I suppose you told her Nicholas was with me?"

"Of course I did." Ivy made a sound of disgust. "I've heard that woman make truly vicious remarks about people, but when she told me Nicholas was shirking his responsibility to Tom by being with you tonight, I told her that was a plain stupid thing to say."

"She probably was upset," Nona said, her mind racing.

"I know she was upset," Ivy said. "But when she told me she intended to take the matter before the church board, I told her to do just that because she would be on a one-woman crusade."

Nona closed her eyes. "I would like to think that was true, Ivy. I really would." she paused. "Are you going to tell Nicholas what Adeline said?"

"I don't think so. I'm sure Adeline doesn't have enough nerve to confront Nicholas openly."

Nona hoped that was true. But the thought of Adeline Drew continuing to gossip about Nicholas behind his back sent a shiver of apprehension down her spine.

"I shouldn't have said anything to you. Now you'll be worried," Ivy said.

"You didn't tell me something I didn't know."

They talked some more before saying goodbye. Nona hung up.

Think of something else for a while, she told herself. Think of the softball game after school tomorrow. Think to remember to tell Mel you'll be gone for a couple of weeks. Think of getting through the next week....

She raised her hand to her heart. It was still beating. She only felt lifeless. Why did it have to be Nicholas?

Nona and Nicholas sat under the shade of an oak, leaning against the trunk as they watched teams of youngsters play softball. Plain bullheadedness had gotten her through the week. She had never allowed self-pity to develop into martyrdom, had never put her emotional suffering on display. And she wasn't going to start now.

When his gaze came to her, she smiled. "I forgot to ask," she said. "How is Tom?"

"He's fine. They thought at first he might have had a heart attack, but it was his ulcers again. How did you know about him, anyway?"

Nona stretched her legs out, ran her fingers down her bare legs, fussed with the knot on her sneaker. "News travels. I'm glad he's doing well," she said at last. "I suppose Adeline was at the hospital."

"Adeline was there." Nicholas shrugged. He forced his gaze from Nona's long legs and studied her profile. What about us, Nona? he wanted to ask.

Her body language was all wrong. She wasn't putting a hand on his chest to shove him away, but she might as well have. She was avoiding his gaze, avoiding contact with him. She was distancing herself before she told him.

The heat of the day and the frustration he was feeling were getting to him, he decided. He was not feeling well. He wiped his brow.

"Nicholas, are you feeling okay?"

THE PERFECT WIFE 163

"Sure. Fine," he said, switching the subject. "I suppose the Beaver Crossing congregation thinks you'll beat us Oak Valleyers in the softball game?"

Nona glanced to where Milly and Jim were sitting a short distance away. "We want to win the softball game, but Milly insists on playing. And she's our weak link," she said in a raised voice.

"She's more than a weak link on the softball team," Jim said.

"I don't know why everyone wants to pick on me," Milly said. She boasted, "I'll bet I'm the only one who can hit a curve ball."

"You won't hit my curve and I'm pitching for Oak Valley," Nicholas said.

Jim hooted. "There you go, Milly."

Milly retorted, "That sounded awfully much like you think you're terrific, Nicholas."

"I am," Nicholas said. "You saw what I did to Nona one-on-one so don't get me mad or I'll wipe you out of the batter's box."

"I am impervious to idle threats," Milly said.

"She is, Nicholas," Jim said. "I threaten her all of the time. It's like water off a duck's back."

"Thank you, Jim," Milly said, faking a sugary tone. "And as for you, Nicholas, I'll hit a home run off the first ball you throw me."

"You'd better watch who you challenge, Milly," Nona said. "Behind Nicholas's nice-guy front, there lurks a really—"

"Now *you* watch it, Nona," Nicholas said. He sighed with relief. Nona, his sweet love was back, the brightness in her eyes shining for him.

"Nicholas! Could you doubt me? I was only going to say there lurks a really, really nice guy behind the nice-guy front."

"You weren't going to say that," Milly retorted. "Go ahead, Nona. Tell us what you really think about Nicholas."

"What can I say? He's—" she nudged him under the chin, "—he's too lovable for words."

Everyone laughed, even Nicholas. But his laughter hid troubling thoughts. When Nona had told him that she would give a hard study to marriage, even if she fell in love, he'd thought she didn't mean it.

But did she? Had she given their relationship a hard study, found it lacking in some way and felt that to nourish it was pointless? Was that why she wouldn't allow him an opening to tell her he loved her. She knew he loved her and she didn't want to hear it?

What had she said about dating? He searched his mind. "It's better to say no at the start than to say no in the middle of a relationship... I allowed myself to be talked into." Something like that.

She had said no in the beginning. And if she said no now, did he have the strength to allow her to act on her convictions, or would he continue to try to convince her that their friendship had only been the tilling of the ground for a lifetime commitment.

The ball game was tied going into the ninth inning and neither team would admit defeat going into the thirteenth.

"I think I've played rather well," Milly said as she and Nona stood on the sidelines watching Cara bat.

"Who ran from the batter's box with the first pitch Nicholas threw?" Nona asked.

"It looked as if it was coming at me."

"You told him you could handle a curve."

"I know why you're siding with Nicholas against me," Milly teased pointedly. "You like him better than you like me."

"Not better," Nona said. She looked at Nicholas, who had moved from pitching to playing third base. He winked. Nona smiled. "Only different."

"Then I'm still your best friend?" Milly asked.

"Sure."

"Liar. Nicholas is your best friend. I know you're telling him all kinds of stuff you'd never trust me with."

Nona laughed, throwing her head back and enjoying it.

"Mission accomplished," Milly said.

"Mission accomplished?"

Milly slipped her arm around Nona's waist and squeezed her. "The tension between you and Nicholas is so thick you could cut it with a knife, as the saying goes. But you managed a laugh, so whatever the problem is, you'll work it through."

"It's complicated, Milly. And getting more so."

"Take it from an expert—me. Love isn't complicated at all." Her gaze went to where Jim was sitting in the bleachers talking to Jenny and Widow Green, who'd ridden with Jenny to the picnic. "We who love make it complicated. Right now, Jim and I are trying to work out a compromise about where we'll live after we get married."

"He thinks near Chicago since his regional office is located there. I want to live in Beaver Crossing, simply because it's the fashion capital of the world." She chuckled. "But we are going to work it out. We won't walk away from what we're feeling. And I have the strangest feeling you want to walk away from Nicholas."

"There's gossip about us. Truly vicious gossip."

"You mean about Adeline Drew catching you and Nicholas in a clinch at the hospital?" Milly said.

Nona gasped. "How long have you known about that?"

"Say a week after it happened. What difference does it make?" Milly asked.

"Adeline is threatening to go to the church council to complain about the time he spends with me," Nona said. She paused, waiting for Cara and Missy, who had approached to either join them or wander away. When they moved on, she said, "He was with me last week when Tom was admitted to the hospital."

Milly sighed in exasperation. "I may be dense—please tell me if I am—but why don't you simply tell Nicholas what Adeline is up to?"

"He doesn't love me. But he's the kind of man who'd feel obligated to defend me and risk losing his church."

Milly patted Nona on the shoulder. "You know I love you, don't you?" Nona nodded. "Well, I've got to tell you. I always thought the one thing I could count on was your intelligence and common sense. But you've just blown your image."

THE PERFECT WIFE

She laughed and looked sorrowful at the same time. "The man loves you, idiot. You love him. Everyone sees that. Everyone's cheering for you. Don't walk away from what you feel for Nicholas, my friend—"

"Miss B.! You're up to bat!" William called.

"I'm coming," Milly yelled. "I feel a home run in me this time." She ran off.

Nona looked at Nicholas. He was standing just off third base, hands on his bare knees just below his shorts. Did he look pale in spite of his tan, or was it the failing daylight?

He had played as spiritedly as everyone else, but there had been times when he'd looked tired to her.

He'd been quiet, pensive. But so had she. Did he love her? Yes. She knew that he did... but it was the same kind of love he had for everyone.

She could take Milly's advice and tell him about Adeline. But she wouldn't. The only peace of mind she would know after this was over would be from the knowledge that she had not come between Nicholas and his church.

It was dark by the time Nicholas pulled the car up in front of Nona's house. As Nona started to get out, he said, "Let's sit here and talk."

"I... don't know. How about a glass of ice tea?" she asked.

"Your mother's car is in the drive. I want to talk to you. You've had a week. And I want to hear what you have to say," he said.

"Mother will wonder what happened to us," Nona said. "I told her we'd be home shortly."

Nicholas knew she was procrastinating. But he wasn't feeling well enough to play games with her. "Your mother won't wonder about us."

He slid across the seat and slipped his arm over her shoulder. She yielded easily and he was comforted by the feel of her. When he bent to kiss her, she said, "Nicholas, someone might see us."

"I don't care. I haven't kissed you in a week." Nicholas ran his lips over her cheek, to her ear, then sought her lips again. She trembled. He caressed her back and arms. Her fingers came to his face.

He deepened the kiss, pulling her closer. When her warm legs touched his, the hot winds of desire blew over him. Didn't she understand? Her lips were made to mate with his; her body to mate with his. And her spirit...

He teased her lips, and they parted with a soft sound.

He could take what he wanted from her physically—but he wouldn't. He wanted to be giving, to make love to her in slow, seductive stages, to learn the secrets of her body while she learned the secrets of his. And he could do that only after they had declared their love and commitment before God.

He wrapped his fingers in her hair, pulled his lips from hers. "Open your eyes, Nona."

"I can't."

"Don't be a coward! Look me in the eye when you tell me what you've decided. Do we go forward? Or are you calling the whole thing off?"

Her lashes fluttered open. He saw a flash of anger.

"I'm not calling our friendship off," she said. "But I don't want to see as much of you as I have been. It's... it's getting uncomfortable for me."

"You're lying!"

"I am not lying!"

He kissed her again, holding back none of the futility he felt. She tried to push him away, and finally he drew back. He was sated, but sickened by his action.

"This time I do apologize, Nona," he said raggedly.

"And you should," she moaned. "Nicholas, what were you trying to prove?"

"That our need for each other goes beyond a physical yearning," he admitted disparagingly.

"I'd like to suggest that was a strange way of proving it," she said, her voice sounding parched.

Nicholas moved away. "I care for you very deeply. You owe me an explanation about what's going on."

She did owe him that. She should tell him what Adeline was saying, and how she knew he did care, but that his feelings for her couldn't be strong enough to survive if she cost him his church. And that she knew nothing could fill the void Corinne had left.

"I know you care deeply about me," she said. "But Corinne—"

"We're not discussing Corinne tonight," Nicholas snapped. "What makes you so fearful of falling in love? That's the issue."

"I am not fearful of falling in love," Nona said. She felt her heart breaking in small pieces with each word they spoke. "But I need someone who can love me without reservation. Corinne was a lucky—"

His glazed look silenced her. "I don't feel up to talking about Corinne right now. All that's relevant is why you're doing this."

"I just told you," Nona said.

"I can love you without reservation," he said. "But you can't seem to love me for what I am."

"I need you as a friend! But you're going to take that away from me if you keep pressing the issue," Nona said. She slipped from the car, shut the door quickly. "I'll...uh...maybe call you when I get back from Iowa City," she said.

She turned and fled, praying she could reach the privacy of her bedroom without her mother seeing her. She couldn't keep up the front anymore.

Nicholas watched Nona open the screen door and step inside. He should go after her. But his head ached. His body ached. He couldn't recall half of their conversation, and the other half he didn't want to recall.

He was beginning to think the unthinkable. She didn't love him. And he was feeling so rotten, he couldn't sort it out right now.

Nicholas leaned back in his chair and closed his eyes. He rubbed his temples. The headache was agonizing, his throat so sore it was difficult to swallow. Whatever he had had the past two weeks wasn't going away. He was going to have to see a doctor.

He opened his eyes when Ivy stepped into the room.

"Our plane tickets home are for next Tuesday," she said as she crossed the room and took the chair opposite him. "You aren't feeling any better, are you?"

"Not much. I'll miss you and Kelly," he said. "But now that you've decided to go back to college, I know you're anxious to get home and settled before school starts for both of you."

"I am looking forward to returning to college. Bill always thought it was a mistake that I didn't finish the year I had left." She smiled.

"You've always loved working with numbers. You'll enjoy being an accountant," he said.

"I know I will," Ivy said. Her brow furrowed. "Don't you think you should see a doctor, Nicholas? You've lost weight. Actually, you look terrible."

Nicholas chuckled. "You know just what to say to make me feel better, don't you?" he asked. Before she could answer, he added, "I'm going to make an appointment Monday."

Ivy smiled, sat back. "Good. Now, are you sure you can get along without me?"

"I'll make the effort."

"I can tell by the way you're grinning at me," Ivy said, "that you think I've been a pain."

"A pain you might be, Ivy, but you're my pain and I love you."

"I know. And I love you." Ivy shifted nervously. "Nicholas...I hesitated to bring this up, but I think I'd be wrong if I didn't."

"Sounds like a cliff-hanger," Nicholas joked.

Ivy smiled. "I—good grief, I don't know how to say this. Straight out, I guess. Nicholas, I think it would be best for both you and Nona if she didn't visit you here after Kelly and I have gone."

Nicholas shook his head. "You've got me. I don't know whether I should laugh or rage at such a suggestion. Why shouldn't Nona visit me in my own home?"

"Get real, will you?" Ivy asked sharply.

"Get real, Ivy? What does that mean?"

"It means Nona is an attractive woman. And she's a divorcée. What do you think some people with small minds might think?"

"I don't care what people think. I know how I feel."

"There is talk, Nicholas. Remember that night Tom Drew was rushed to the hospital?"

"Of course I remember. You were waiting up to tell me Adeline had called."

Ivy sighed. "Naturally, Adeline asked for you. Without giving it a moment's thought, I told her you were at Nona's but I'd contact you," she said. "Adeline got huffy. One word led to another and she threatened to go to the church board to complain that because of Nona, you're neglecting the people in your church."

Nicholas sighed heavily. Nona had made the right call on Adeline. "I doubt if she'll follow through."

"I'm afraid of what she'll do if she hears Nona's been visiting you here after Kelly and I leave."

Slowly the puzzle of Nona's behavior started to come together. "So you called Nona that night, but I'd left?"

"You were on the way home. I was still so angry with Adeline that I'm afraid I told Nona what Ade-

THE PERFECT WIFE

line said. But she'd already heard. The Alexanders had told her."

Of course, Nicholas thought. Nona had had lunch with the Alexanders that Sunday. Now her actions made sense. She was trying to shield him from gossip by distancing herself from him. She loved him that much.

"I don't know why you're smiling," Ivy said. "But you won't be smiling long because there's more. And it's worse."

"There's more?" Nicholas felt torn between laughter and tears. "And it's worse?"

Ivy slapped her hand on the desk. "She said there was *something* going on between you and Nona!"

"And you said?" Nicholas asked. Ivy's eyes were wide. She was furious.

"And I said, 'You don't know what you're talking about Adeline!'" Ivy paused for a breath then narrowed her eyes. "And Adeline said 'I saw him kissing the woman myself. With my very own eyes. And that's being disrespectful of his dead wife.'"

"That's the worst?" Nicholas asked.

Ivy leaned back, blushing. "No. I'm afraid I was furious, like I said. And, uh, I told her she wouldn't know what a kiss was if she saw one."

"You didn't." Nicholas laughed. This was the Ivy he'd grown up with. With backbone, who rightly or wrongly would stand up for herself.

"I did," Ivy said.

"You shouldn't have," Nicholas offered.

"I know. And I told her there was not one thing going on between you and Nona."

"About that you were wrong," Nicholas said.

"I was wrong?" Ivy asked, looking very surprised.

"A lot has been going on between Nona and myself. And I hope for a lot more between us." He sighed. "I have something to tell you, Ivy. About Corinne."

Chapter Twelve

Nona paced the kitchen, glancing at her mother everytime she passed the chair where Jenny sat.

"Nona! Will you stop that pacing! You're making me feel like I'm testifying before a grand jury." She paused. "I told you! I don't know what's wrong with Nicholas."

"Emily—"

"I told you Emily didn't know either. She called to ask you if you'd heard what was wrong with him," Jenny said sounding short. "Stop that pacing!"

Nona walked to the table, pulled out a chair. Plopped. "I'm not pacing."

"All right," Jenny said. "This is the last time I'm explaining it. Emily called. Nicholas sickened during his sermon this morning. Ivy took him to the hospital. I tried calling Ivy. No one answers. I suppose she's still at the hospital.''

"He sickened this morning during the church service and Ivy took him to the hospital," Nona said. She was numb with shock. She remembered how pale, yet flushed he'd been at the softball game. How tired he'd looked. How warm his face and lips had been when they kissed.

"That's all I know," Jenny said calmly. "It's probably nothing much."

Nona exploded from the chair. "Mother! How can you say that? If he collapsed during his sermon, he has to be very sick."

Jenny eyed Nona warily. "Emily didn't say he collapsed. She said he sickened during his sermon. She also said she and Jon, Sr. had seen him last night and he'd looked a little drawn, but otherwise all right."

"I'm going to call Ivy. She might be home by now."

"That's exactly—" Nona was already dialing "—what I thought," Jenny said. "You aren't listening to me."

"It's ringing," Nona said. "Come on, Ivy! Answer—"

"Reverend Kendrick's residence. Ivy speaking."

"Ivy! This is Nona. I'm so glad you're home."

"I got here an hour ago, but between telephone calls and people dropping in to ask about Nicholas, I haven't had a chance to call you. He wanted me to call you right away."

"What's wrong with him?"

"He's going to undergo surgery, maybe tomorrow, but definitely sometime this week. Or as soon as they can—My goodness. Someone's at the door. Can I call you right back?"

Nona almost stamped her foot in frustration. "Of course," she said sounding calm. "Call as—"

"Nona, this isn't a good time to bring this up, but I have to set something straight with you. All the talking I did about Corinne, the impression I gave that she was a perfect helpmate for Nicholas—I was wrong," Ivy's voice broke. She sniffled.

"Ivy! What's wrong with him?" Nona demanded, but Ivy went on as if she hadn't heard. "I'm afraid my constant talking caused real trouble between you and Nicholas."

"What's—"

"I hope it's not too late for you and Nicholas. Oh, blast. The doorbell."

The phone slammed in Nona's ear. She stared at the handset, thinking horrible thoughts.

She hung up, then turned to her mother. "As soon as I freshen up, I'm going to Sioux City," she said.

"My goodness."

Nona glanced at the clock. Seven-thirty. If she hurried, she could make it before visiting hours were over at nine. "He's undergoing surgery tomorrow or sometime this week."

"What kind of surgery?"

Nona quickly explained how Ivy had been called to the door so she didn't know anymore than that Nicholas had wanted Ivy to call her. He had to want to see her, so she was going.

"You don't even know which hospital he's at. Oh, go change clothes. The Alexander answering service will call the hospitals and check."

Nona kissed her mother's cheek. "Thank you."

"Nicholas is the picture of health," Jenny said. "I'm sure it's nothing serious."

"Dad was the picture of health, too," Nona whispered.

"He was," Jenny said softly. "But we had known for several years about his heart problem. Nowadays, there would have been something the doctors could do. Don't stand around listening to me get morbid. Go to Nicholas. He's going to be fine, Nona."

Nona smiled gratefully. She needed comforting. But until she saw Nicholas, knew what was wrong and what could be done to fix it, not even her mother's love was comfort enough.

"I hope it's not too late for you and Nicholas."

Ivy's words banged around in Nona's head as she drove to Sioux City and by the time she'd parked, she was convinced Nicholas was gravely ill.

Minutes later she was in the hospital elevator, pushing the button for Nicholas's floor. The door closed with aggravating slowness. She didn't have time for this! Every second counted. She'd wasted too much time already.

On Nicholas's floor she squeezed through the elevator doors before they'd completely opened. She raced down the hall toward his room.

The door was open. He was sitting up in bed, reaching for the telephone. He was hooked to an intravenous feeding tube.

He was pale and since she'd last seen him he'd lost so much weight his cheekbones, always prominent, were even more so, making his cheeks appear sunken.

In spite of what she had been thinking, she had held out hope that he wasn't sick. Even though he had admitted he was vulnerable she had believed he was invulnerable. In her mind, his strength was limitless...but now his vulnerability was etched in his face. He needed her.

And what he needed was her strength, her support. Not weeping and wailing. So she struggled to hold back her tears, then threw back her shoulders and put a smile on her face.

He must have sensed her presence because he looked toward the door smiling. "I was just going to call you," he said. He returned the handset to the cradle. "How did the seminar go?"

Nona's preparation was for nothing. She couldn't make idle conversation. She rushed inside only vaguely aware that she passed one bed to get to Nicholas.

She threw her arms around him. "Oh, Nicholas," she murmured. "Nicholas." She pressed her lips against his.

When she pulled back, he whispered, "I think you missed me."

"I don't know whether she missed you or not," a voice said from the next bed. "But I know one thing. No one kissed me like that when I had my tonsils out."

Nona sat on the edge of the bed, glanced at the blond-haired man who'd spoken, then turned back to Nicholas. "You're going to have your tonsils out?" she asked, confused.

"Something I should have done years ago, but I guess this is it," Nicholas said.

Nona pointed to the I.V., still not quite convinced. "What's that I.V. for?"

"I'm being pumped full of antibiotics. As soon as the infection is under control, they'll do the surgery."

Relief flowed through Nona's veins and surfaced in a tear. Nicholas wiped it away. "What's this all about?" he asked.

"I thought—oh, forget it."

"You thought I was terminal?"

"Something like that."

"Didn't Ivy call you?"

"I talked to her. She told me you were going to have surgery but before she could say what for, someone came to the door. Then she started crying." Nona shrugged. "She said she was sorry because she'd given me the wrong impression...and she hoped it wasn't too late for us."

"I know what Ivy was talking about," Nicholas said. "But I was the guilty one, not Ivy. Ivy didn't know about—" He drew his knees up. "I'm getting out of bed. We need to talk. If I remember correctly, there's a small consultation room off the visitors' waiting room."

"What about the I.V.?" Nona asked.

"I'm ambulatory. I take the rig with me wherever I go."

Nona assisted him with his robe. He placed his hand on the small of Nona's back and ushered her toward the door. "See you later, Alex," Nicholas said.

"Don't hurry." Alex grinned. "Bed check isn't until eleven."

Once out of the room, Nona asked, "Do you need a hand with that rig?"

"I need a hand, but not with the rig. I need your hand," he said.

She took the hand he offered. Fingers entwined, they maneuvered down the hall to the small consultation room. Nicholas sat on the sofa and pulled Nona down beside him. He slipped his arm around her, kissing the tip of her nose, her lips, her chin in quick succession.

"I love you, Nicholas. More than life, I love you," she murmured.

"And you, Nona, are the only love I have ever known. The only love."

"It shouldn't have come to this. My thinking you were dying before I could tell you I loved you," she said. "Pretty stupid of me, huh?"

"Nearly as stupid as I've been," Nicholas said, touching her trembling lip with a fingertip. "My guilt over Corinne's death kept me from admitting my love, because I knew the moment I admitted it, I'd have to admit the kind of man I am. How much did Ivy tell you about Corinne?"

"Only that she wasn't the perfect helpmate I'd believed," Nona said. "But I know what kind of man you are, Nicholas—kind, loving and compassionate."

"Let me talk, Nona. Then see if you still agree." He hesitated, then very quietly he told Nona about his marriage, holding back none of the good and none of the bad. He watched her expression flash anger and disbelief. Then compassion and sorrow when he told her about Corinne's refusing to have a family.

He ended with the night Corinne died, got as far as his demand that they get help or the marriage was over when his voice broke from the raw pain he was feeling.

Nona stroked his hand, whispered, "I love you, Nicholas."

He smiled weakly, but strengthened by her words, he concluded. "Corinne said I wouldn't get the chance. She was leaving. When her car ended wrapped around a tree, everyone assumed it was an accident. But I knew it might not have been an accident. I knew I might have been guilty of driving her into taking her life."

"Nicholas," Nona said softly, "you were trying to save your marriage, not end it."

"I spoke the words, Nona. But I didn't know in my heart whether or not I wanted the marriage saved. And... when she told me I wouldn't get the chance to walk, that she would leave me—" His voice broke. He felt his tears flowing. "I told her to go. I never wanted to see her again."

Nona tried to reach for him. He held her away. "Don't you understand, Nona? She was right!" He swiped at his tears. "I didn't love her. I never did. Not the way she needed to be loved. Our marriage was a lie, a pretense we maintained for the sake of my ministry." He bit back his tears. "Now do you think you know me?" he demanded softly. "Do you?"

Nona's eyes welled with tears, but her voice was strong. "I know you so well that I know you had love in your heart for Corinne. Had she loved you, your love for her would have grown, not died."

"But even if she wasn't loving, I should have shown her compassion," Nicholas said.

"How many times have you told me that you aren't perfect, Nicholas? What you are is a man of God. You aren't God. You aren't perfect. But you are my love and I love you."

Then holding each other, they cried unashamedly and wiped each other's tears.

When the tears were spent, Nicholas kissed her temple. "I'll still have times when I doubt myself."

"And I'll have times of doubting, but we'll have each other—"

"That sounds as if you intend to marry me," Nicholas said. "Will you?"

Nona withdrew to arm's length. "Before we can discuss that, I have to tell you about Adeline Drew."

"Ivy told me what Adeline was threatening to do," he said. "That's what was behind your sudden change of heart, wasn't it? You'd heard about Adeline's threat and were trying to protect me."

Nona nodded.

"The matter is settled. I called a council meeting last night. I invited Adeline and the Alexanders. I told them it had come to my attention that there was some question about ethics of my dating you."

Nona gasped. Nicholas hugged her close. "Adeline had her opening. She took it, saying, 'Reverend Kendrick. Your conduct is not becoming to a minister. It is disgraceful.'"

"I explained that before coming to Oak Valley, I'd considered giving up the ministry, but because you'd given me the kind of love and support I needed in a time of crisis, my faith in myself had been renewed. I was a better person, better able to minister."

"What did Adeline say to that?"

"She said, 'No matter how you feel about *that* woman, you are being disrespectful of your wife.'"

"I'm so sorry, Nicholas. It had to be embarrassing for you."

"I didn't find it embarrassing at all. I told Adeline I intended to ask you to be my wife. At that point, Ivy, who had been quiet for all of ten minutes, put in a few hundred words, more or less, in support of us. Then Emily and Jon Sr. jumped in. He asked where it was written that a minister wasn't supposed to be happy. Emily gave a fine sermon on charity of action and thought."

"It almost turned into a fiasco," Nicholas said. "One of the board members suggested that if Adeline was unhappy with me, she should consider looking for membership in another church. I couldn't let that go on. I reminded everyone we were members of the same church family, that you don't disown family, you try to understand them. I believe Adeline was shocked into realizing how she'd been acting."

Nicholas ended with a smile, but his eyes were moist again. "I have never been defended with such purpose, never felt so surrounded by love."

"And I want to surround you with more love," Nona whispered. "Yes, I'll marry you. When?"

"As soon as I get this little episode with my tonsils—" he paused when the expression in Nona's eyes grew mischievous. "Don't laugh. My throat is darn sore."

He kissed the wickedness out of her and when she was pliant and unresisting, asked, "How about next Sunday?"

"I'd love to, but knowing Milly, she'll need longer than a week to pick out the right dress to wear as maid of honor."

"Let's not talk about Milly. Let's talk about me."

"What about you?"

"I feel weak, feverish. I think I'm having a relapse. Did you learn anything at the seminar that might be used as emergency treatment?"

"How about the old surefire cure for bad hurts," Nona suggested with a grin.

"You're wasting time, my darling wife-to-be. Get to it."

"Gladly," Nona said, kissing him. "Happily." She kissed him again. "Joyously."

"And through eternity," Nicholas murmured, kissing her.

"Amen," Nona whispered against his cherished lips. "Amen."

* * * * *

Silhouette Romance

COMING NEXT MONTH

#688 FATHER CHRISTMAS—Mary Blayney
Daniel Marshall had never thought he could have it all: his precious daughters *and* the woman who'd given them a mother's love. But Annie VerHollan believed in Christmas miracles....

#689 DREAM AGAIN OF LOVE—Phyllis Halldorson
Mary Beth Warren had left her husband, Flynn, upon discovering the truth behind their vows. Now that they had a second chance, could she risk dreaming again of love?

#690 MAKE ROOM FOR NANNY—Carol Grace
Maggie Chisholm planned to faithfully abide by her nanny handbook. But the moment she laid eyes on Garrett Townsend she broke the golden rule—by falling in love with her boss!

#691 MAKESHIFT MARRIAGE—Janet Franklin
Practical Brad Williamson had proposed to Rachel Carson purely for the sake of her orphaned niece and nephew. But how long could Rachel conceal her longing for more than a makeshift marriage?

#692 TEN DAYS IN PARADISE—Karen Leabo
Carrie Bishop arrived in St. Thomas seeking adventure and found it while hunting for treasure with Jack Harrington. But she never counted on the handsome loner being her most priceless find....

#693 SWEET ADELINE—Sharon De Vita
Adeline Simpson had gone to Las Vegas to find her grandfather and bring him back home. Could casino owner Mac Cole convince lovely Addy that she was missing a lot more?

AVAILABLE THIS MONTH:

#682 RUN, ISABELLA
Suzanne Carey

#683 THE PERFECT WIFE
Marcine Smith

#684 SWEET PROTECTOR
Patricia Ellis

#685 THIEF OF HEARTS
Beverly Terry

#686 MOTHER FOR HIRE
Marie Ferrarella

#687 FINALLY HOME
Arlene James

Silhouette Special Edition

MORE SPECIAL THAN EVER, SAY THESE TOP AUTHORS:

LINDA HOWARD

"Silhouette Special Editions are indeed 'special' to me. They reflect the complexity of the modern woman's life, professionally, emotionally and, of course, romantically. They are windows through which we can see different views of life, the means by which we can experience all the depths and altitudes of the great love we want and need in our lives. Silhouette Special Editions are special dreams; we need dreams—to take us out of our everyday lives, and to give us something to reach for."

EMILIE RICHARDS

"I write stories about love and lovers because I believe we can't be reminded too often that love changes lives. I write Silhouette Special Editions because longer, in-depth stories give me the chance to explore all love's aspects, from the mad whirl to the quiet moments of contemplation. There's nothing more special than love, and there's no line more special than Silhouette Special Edition. I am proud to tell my stories in its pages."

READERS' COMMENTS ON SILHOUETTE ROMANCES:

"The best time of my day is when I put my children to bed at naptime and sit down to read a Silhouette Romance. Keep up the good work."
—P.M.*, Allegan, MI

"I am very fond of the quality of your Silhouette Romances. They are so real. I have tried to read some of the other romances, but I always come back to Silhouette."
—C.S., Mechanicsburg, PA

"I feel that Silhouette Books offer a wider choice and/or variety than any of the other romance books available."
—R.R., Aberdeen, WA

"I have enjoyed reading Silhouette Romances for many years now. They are light and refreshing. You can always put yourself in the main characters' place, feeling alive and beautiful."
—J.M.K., San Antonio, TX

"My boyfriend always teases me about Silhouette Books. He asks me, how's my love life and naturally I say terrific, but I tell him that there is always room for a little more romance from Silhouette."
—F.N., Ontario, Canada

*names available on request

You'll flip... your pages won't!
Read paperbacks *hands-free* with

Book Mate · I

The perfect "mate" for all your romance paperbacks

Traveling • Vacationing • At Work • In Bed • Studying • Cooking • Eating

Perfect size for all standard paperbacks, this wonderful invention makes reading a pure pleasure! Ingenious design holds paperback books OPEN and FLAT so even wind can't ruffle pages— leaves your hands free to do other things. Reinforced, wipe-clean vinyl-covered holder flexes to let you turn pages without undoing the strap... supports paperbacks so well, they have the strength of hardcovers!

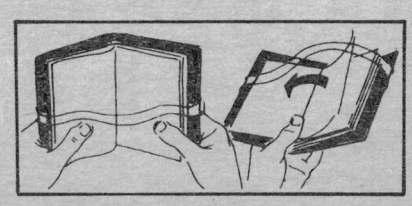

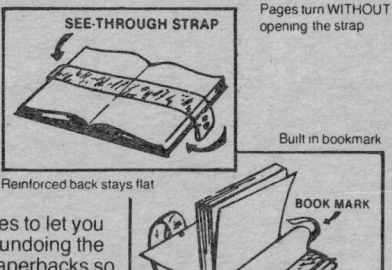

Pages turn WITHOUT opening the strap

SEE-THROUGH STRAP

Reinforced back stays flat

Built in bookmark

BOOK MARK

BACK COVER HOLDING STRIP

10 x 7¼ opened.
Snaps closed for easy carrying, too

Available now. Send your name, address, and zip code, along with a check or money order for just $5.95 + .75¢ for postage & handling (for a total of $6.70) payable to Reader Service to:

Reader Service
Bookmate Offer
901 Fuhrmann Blvd.
P.O. Box 1396
Buffalo, N.Y. 14269-1396

Offer not available in Canada
*New York and Iowa residents add appropriate sales tax.

BM-G

Available now from
SILHOUETTE Desire

TAGGED #534
by Lass Small

Fredricka Lambert had always believed in true love, but she couldn't figure out whom to love... until lifelong friend Colin Kilgallon pointed her in the right direction—toward himself.

Fredricka is one of five fascinating Lambert sisters. She is as enticing as each one of her four sisters, whose stories you have already enjoyed.

- Hillary in GOLDILOCKS AND THE BEHR (Desire #437)
- Tate in HIDE AND SEEK (Desire #453)
- Georgina in RED ROVER (Desire #491)
- Roberta in ODD MAN OUT (Desire #505)

Don't miss the last book of this enticing miniseries, only from Silhouette Desire.

If you missed any of the Lambert sisters' stories by Lass Small, send $2.50 plus 75 cents postage and handling to:

In the U.S.	In Canada
901 Fuhrmann Blvd.	P.O. Box 609
Box 1396	Fort Erie, Ontario
Buffalo, NY 14269-1396	L2A 5X3

SD528-1R

Wonderful, luxurious gifts can be yours with proofs-of-purchase from any specially marked "Indulge A Little" Harlequin or Silhouette book with the Offer Certificate properly completed, plus a check or money order (do not send cash) to cover postage and handling payable to Harlequin/Silhouette "Indulge A Little, Give A Lot" Offer. We will send you the specified gift.

Mail-in-Offer

OFFER CERTIFICATE

Item:	A. Collector's Doll	B. Soaps in a Basket	C. Potpourri Sachet	D. Scented Hangers
# of Proofs-of-Purchase	18	12	6	4
Postage & Handling	$3.25	$2.75	$2.25	$2.00
Check One				

Name _____
Address _____ Apt. # _____
City _____ State _____ Zip _____

ONE PROOF OF PURCHASE

Indulge A Little — GIVE A LOT

To collect your free gift by mail you must include the necessary number of proofs-of-purchase plus postage and handling with offer certificate.

SR-2

Harlequin®/Silhouette®

Mail this certificate, designated number of proofs-of-purchase and check or money order for postage and handling to:

INDULGE A LITTLE
P.O. Box 9055
Buffalo, N.Y. 14269-9055